King of the Grizzlies

He had never seen a bees' nest like this . . . (*see page* 7)

King of the Grizzlies

Two Stories by Ernest Thompson Seton

Illustrated with colour plates by
Mirko Hanák
and line drawings in the text by the author

London: J. M. Dent & Sons Ltd
New York: E. P. Dutton & Co. Inc.

ERNEST THOMPSON SETON was born on 14th August 1860 at South Shields, Durham, one of a family of fourteen. When he was six they emigrated to Canada, first to Lindsay, Ontario, then settling in Toronto. Returning to Lindsay for a summer in 1875 gave him the setting and many of the adventures for his greatest book, 'Two Little Savages' (1903), and from thenceforward Seton devoted himself to nature study. Later he became Naturalist to the Government of Manitoba and author of the standard work 'Life Histories of Northern Animals' (1909). Besides this he was founder of the Woodcraft Movement which was soon amalgamated with the Scout Movement, and he became Chief Scout of America.

As early as 1884 Seton began contributing short accounts of the true adventures of actual animals to various magazines, and his authentic account of how he trapped Lobo, the great wolf of Currumpaw, appeared in 'Scribner's' in 1894. In 1898 he collected the best of these animal biographies as 'Wild Animals I Have Known', which became a best-seller immediately and brought him world-wide renown. He followed it with many excellent stories, long or short, of animal heroes, the most notable being 'The Trail of the Sandhill Stag' (1899), 'The Biography of a Grizzly' (1900), 'Lives of the Hunted' (1901), 'Monarch The Big Bear' (1904) and 'Bannertail: the Story of a Grey Squirrel' (1922).

Besides 'Two Little Savages' (1903) Seton wrote another tale of backwoods adventure, 'Rolf in the Woods' (1911); and his admirable autobiography, 'Trail of an Artist-Naturalist' (1951), was published some years after his death in 1946.

First published in this edition 1972. © Colour illustrations J. M. Dent & Sons Ltd, 1972. All rights reserved. No part of this publication may be reproduced, stored in a retrieval system, or transmitted, in any form or by any means, electronic, mechanical, photocopying, recording or otherwise, without the prior permission of J. M. Dent & Sons Ltd. Made in Great Britain at the Aldine Press, Letchworth, Herts, for J. M. Dent & Sons Ltd, Aldine House, Bedford Street, London. ISBN 0 460 05092 3

Contents

Colour Plates

Monarch the Big Bear

1

The Two Springs

HIGH above Sierra's peaks stands grim Mount Tallac. Ten thousand feet above the sea it rears its head to gaze out north to that vast and wonderful turquoise that men call Lake Tahoe, and north-west, across a piney sea, to its great white sister, Shasta of the Snows; wonderful colours and things on every side, mast-like pine trees strung with jewelry, streams that a Buddhist would have made sacred, hills that an Arab would have held holy. But Lan Kellyan's keen grey eyes were turned to other things. The childish delight in life and light for their own sakes had faded, as they must in one whose training had been to make him hold them very cheap. Why value grass? All the world is grass. Why value air, when it is everywhere in measureless immensity? Why value life, when, all alive, his living came from taking life? His senses were alert, not for the rainbow hills and the gem-bright lakes, but for the living things that he must meet in daily rivalry, each staking on the game, his life. Hunter was written on his leathern garb, on his tawny face, on his lithe and sinewy form, and shone in his clear grey eye.

The cloven granite peak might pass unmarked, but a faint

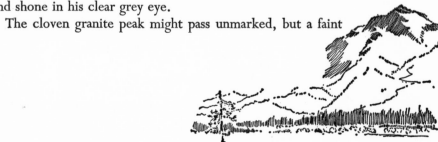

dimple in the sod did not. Calipers could not have told that it was widened at one end, but the hunter's eye did, and following, he looked for and found another, then smaller signs, and he knew that a big bear and two little ones had passed and were still close at hand, for the grass in the marks was yet unbending. Lan rode his hunting pony on the trail. It sniffed and stepped nervously, for it knew as well as the rider that a Grizzly family was near. They came to a terrace leading to an open upland. Twenty feet on this side of it Lan slipped to the ground, dropped the reins, the well-known sign to the pony that he must stand at that spot, then cocked his rifle and climbed the bank. At the top he went with yet greater caution, and soon saw an old Grizzly with her two cubs. She was lying down some fifty yards away and afforded a poor shot; he fired at what seemed to be the shoulder. The aim was true, but the bear got only a flesh-wound. She sprang to her feet and made for the place where the puff of smoke arose. The bear had fifty yards to cover, the man had fifteen, but she came racing down the bank before he was fairly on the horse, and for a hundred yards the pony bounded in terror while the old Grizzly ran almost alongside, striking at him and missing by a scant hair's-breadth each time. But the Grizzly rarely keeps up its great speed for many yards. The horse got under full headway, and the shaggy mother, falling behind, gave up the chase and returned to her cubs.

She was a singular old bear. She had a large patch of white on her breast, white cheeks and shoulders, graded into the brown elsewhere, and Lan from this remembered her afterwards as the 'Pinto.' She had almost caught him that time, and the hunter was ready to believe that he owed her a grudge.

A week later his chance came. As he passed along the rim of Pocket Gulch, a small, deep valley with sides of sheer rock in most places, he saw afar the old Pinto bear with her two

little brown cubs. She was crossing from one side where the wall was low to another part easy to climb. As she stopped to drink at the clear stream Lan fired with his rifle. At the shot Pinto turned on her cubs, and slapping first one, then the other, she chased them up a tree. Now a second shot struck her and she charged fiercely up the sloping part of the wall, clearly recognizing the whole situation and determined to destroy that hunter. She came snorting up the steep acclivity wounded and raging, only to receive a final shot in the brain that sent her rolling back to lie dead at the bottom of Pocket Gulch. The hunter, after waiting to make sure, moved to the edge and fired another shot into the old one's body; then reloading, he went cautiously down to the tree where still were the cubs. They gazed at him with wild seriousness as he approached them, and when he began to climb they scrambled up higher. Here one set up a plaintive whining and the other an angry growling, their outcries increasing as he came nearer.

He took out a stout cord, and noosing them in turn, dragged them to the ground. One rushed at him and, though little bigger than a cat, would certainly have done him serious injury had he not held it off with a forked stick. After tying them to a strong but swaying branch he went to his horse, got a grain-bag, dropped them into that, and rode with them to his shanty. He fastened each with a collar and chain to a post, up which they climbed, and sitting on the top they whined and growled, according to their humour. For the first few days there was danger of the cubs strangling themselves or of starving to death, but at length they were beguiled into drinking some milk most ungently procured from a range cow that was lassoed for the purpose. In another week they seemed somewhat reconciled to their lot, and thenceforth plainly notified their captor whenever they wanted food or water.

And thus the two small rills ran on, a little farther down the mountain now, deeper and wider, keeping near each other; leaping bars, rejoicing in the sunlight, held for a while by some trivial dam, but overleaping that and running on with pools and deeps that harbour bigger things.

The Springs and
the Miner's Dam

J ACK and Jill, the hunter named the cubs; and Jill, the little fury, did nothing to change his early impression of her bad temper. When at food time the man came she would get as far as possible up the post and growl, or else sit in sulky fear and silence; Jack would scramble down and strain at his chain to meet his captor, whining softly, and gobbling his food at once with the greatest of gusto and the worst of manners. He had many odd ways of his own, and he was a lasting rebuke to those who say an animal has no sense of humour. In a month he had grown so tame that he was allowed to run free. He followed his master like a dog, and his tricks and funny doings were a continual delight to Kellyan and the few friends he had in the mountains.

On the creek-bottom below the shack was a meadow where Lan cut enough hay each year to feed his two ponies through the winter. This year when hay time came Jack was his daily companion, either following him about in dangerous nearness to the snorting scythe, or curling up an hour at a time on his coat to guard it assiduously from such aggressive monsters as ground squirrels and chipmunks. An interesting variation of the day came about whenever the mower found a bumblebees' nest. Jack loved honey, of course, and knew quite well what a bees' nest was, so the call, 'Honey—Jacky—honey!' never failed to bring him in waddling haste to the spot. Jerking his nose up in token of pleasure, he would approach cautiously, for he knew that bees have stings. Watching his chance, he would dexterously slap at them with his paws till, one by one, they were knocked down and crushed; then sniffing hard for the latest information, he would stir up the nest gingerly till the very last was tempted forth to be killed. When the dozen or more that formed the swarm were thus got rid of, Jack would carefully dig out the nest and eat first the honey, next the grubs and wax, and last of all the bees he had killed, champing his jaws like a little pig at a trough, while his long red, snaky tongue was ever busy lashing the stragglers into his greedy maw.

Lan's nearest neighbour was Lou Bonamy, an ex-cowboy and sheep-herder, now a prospecting miner. He lived, with his dog, in a shanty about a mile below Kellyan's shack. Bonamy had seen Jack 'perform on a bee-crew.' And one day as he came to Kellyan's, he called out: 'Lan, bring Jack here and we'll have some fun.' He led the way down the stream into the woods. Kellyan followed him, and Jacky waddled at Kellyan's heels, sniffing once in a while to make sure he was not follow- the wrong pair of legs.

'There, Jacky, honey—honey!' and Bonamy pointed up a tree to an immense wasps' nest.

Jack cocked his head on one side and swung his nose on the other. Certainly those things buzzing about looked like bees, though he never before saw a bees' nest of that shape, or in such a place.

But he scrambled up the trunk. The men waited—Lan in doubt as to whether he should let his pet cub go into such danger, Bonamy insisting it would be a capital joke 'to spring

a surprise' on the little bear. Jack reached the branch that held the big nest high over the deep water, but went with increasing caution. He had never seen a bees' nest like this; it did not have the right smell. Then he took another step forward on the branch—what an awful lot of bees; another step—still they were undoubtedly bees; he cautiously advanced a foot—and bees mean honey; a little farther—he was now within four feet of the great paper globe. The bees hummed angrily and Jack stepped back, in doubt. The men giggled; then Bonamy called softly and untruthfully: 'Honey—Jacky—honey!'

The little bear, fortunately for himself, went slowly, since in doubt; he made no sudden move, and he waited a long time, though urged to go on, till the whole swarm of bees had re-entered their nest. Now Jacky jerked his nose up, hitched softly out a little farther till right over the fateful paper globe He reached out, and by lucky chance put one horny little paw-pad over the hole; his other arm grasped the nest, and leaping from the branch he plunged headlong into the pool below, taking the whole thing with him. As soon as he reached the water his hind feet were seen tearing into the nest, kicking it to pieces; then he let it go and struck out for the shore, the nest floating in rags down-stream. He ran alongside till the comb lodged against a shallow place, then he plunged in again; the wasps were drowned or too wet to be dangerous, and he carried his prize to the bank in triumph. No honey; of course, that was a disappointment, but there were lots of fat white grubs—almost as good—and Jack ate till his paunch looked like a little rubber balloon.

'How is that?' chuckled Lan.

'The laugh is on us,' answered Bonamy, with a grimace.

3

The Trout Pool

JACK was now growing into a sturdy cub, and he would
follow Kellyan even as far as Bonamy's shack. One day, as
they watched him rolling head over heels in riotous glee,
Kellyan remarked to his friend: 'I'm afraid some one will
happen on him an' shoot him in the woods for a wild b'ar.'

'Then why don't you earmark him with them thar new
sheep-rings?' was the sheep-man's suggestion.

Thus it was that, much against his will, Jack's ears were
punched and he was decorated with earrings like a prize ram.
The intention was good, but they were neither ornamental nor
comfortable. Jack fought them for days, and when at length
he came home trailing a branch that was caught in the jewel
of his left ear, Kellyan impatiently removed them.

At Bonamy's he formed two new acquaintances, a blustering,
bullying old ram that was 'in storage' for a sheep-herder
acquaintance, and which inspired him with a lasting enmity for
everything that smelt of sheep—and Bonamy's dog.

This latter was an active, yapping, unpleasant cur that
seemed to think it rare fun to snap at Jacky's heels, then bound
out of reach. A joke is a joke, but this horrid beast did not

know where to stop, and Jack's first and second visits to the Bonamy hut were quite spoiled by the tyranny of the dog. If Jack could have got hold of him he might have settled the account to his own satisfaction, but he was not quick enough for that. His only refuge was up a tree. He soon discovered that he was happier away from Bonamy's, and thenceforth when he saw his protector take the turn that led to the miner's cabin, Jack said plainly with a look, 'No, thank you,' and turned back to amuse himself at home.

His enemy, however, often came with Bonamy to the hunter's cabin, and there resumed his amusement of teasing the little bear. It proved so interesting a pursuit that the dog learned to come over on his own account whenever he felt like having some fun, until at length Jack was kept in continual terror of the yellow cur. But it all ended very suddenly.

One hot day, while the two men smoked in front of Kellyan's house, the dog chased Jack up a tree and then stretched himself out for a pleasant nap in the shade of its branches. Jack was forgotten as the dog slumbered. The little bear kept very quiet for a while, then, as his twinkling brown eyes came back to that hateful dog, that he could neither catch nor get away from, an idea seemed to grow in his small brain. He began to move slowly and silently down the branch until he was over the foe, slumbering, twitching his limbs, and making little sounds that told of dreams of the chase, or, more likely, dreams of tormenting a helpless bear cub. Of course, Jack knew nothing of that. His one thought, doubtless, was that he hated that cur and now he could vent his hate. He came just over the tyrant, and taking careful aim, he jumped and landed squarely on the dog's ribs. It was a terribly rude awakening, but the dog gave no yelp, for the good reason that the breath was knocked out of his body. No bones were broken, though he was barely able to drag himself away in silent defeat, while Jacky played a lively tune on his rear with paws that were fringed with meat-hooks.

Evidently it was a most excellent plan; and when the dog came around after that, or when Jack went to Bonamy's with his master, as he soon again ventured to do, he would scheme with more or less success to 'get the drop on the purp,' as the men put it. The dog now rapidly lost interest in bear-baiting, and in a short time it was a forgotten sport.

4

The Stream that Sank in the Sand

JACK was funny; Jill was sulky. Jack was petted and given freedom, so grew funnier; Jill was beaten and chained, so grew sulkier. She had a bad name and she was often punished for it; it is usually so.

One day, while Lan was away, Jill got free and joined her brother. They broke into the little storehouse and rioted among the provisions. They gorged themselves with the choicest sorts; and the common stuffs, like flour, butter, and baking-powder, brought fifty miles on horseback, were good enough only to be thrown about the ground or rolled in. Jack had just torn open the last bag of flour, and Jill was puzzling over a box of miner's dynamite, when the doorway darkened and there stood Kellyan, a picture of amazement and wrath. Little bears do not know anything about pictures, but they have some acquaintance with wrath. They seemed to know that they were sinning, or at least in danger, and Jill sneaked, sulky and snuffy, into a dark corner, where she glared defiantly at the hunter. Jack put his head on one side, then, quite forgetful of all his misbehaviour, he gave

a delighted grunt, and scuttling towards the man, he whined, jerked his nose, and held up his sticky, greasy arms to be lifted and petted as though he were the best little bear in the world.

Alas, how likely we are to be taken at our own estimate! The scowl faded from the hunter's brow as the cheeky and deplorable little bear began to climb his leg. 'You little divil,' he growled, 'I'll break your cussed neck.' But he did not. He lifted the nasty, sticky little beast and fondled him as usual, while Jill, no worse—even more excusable, because less trained—suffered all the terrors of his wrath and was double-chained to the post, so as to have no further chance of such ill-doing.

This was a day of bad luck for Kellyan. That morning he had fallen and broken his rifle. Now, on his return home, he found his provisions spoiled, and a new trial was before him.

A stranger with a small pack-train called at his place that evening and passed the night with him. Jack was in his most frolicsome mood and amused them both with tricks half-puppy and half-monkey like, and in the morning, when the stranger was leaving, he said: 'Say, pard, I'll give you twenty-five dollars for the pair.' Lan hesitated, thought of the wasted provisions, his empty purse, his broken rifle, and answered: 'Make it fifty and it's a go.'

'Shake on it.'

So the bargain was made, the money paid, and in fifteen minutes the stranger was gone with a little bear in each pannier of his horse.

Jill was surly and silent; Jack kept up a whining that smote on Lan's heart with a reproachful sound, but he braced himself with, 'Guess they're better out of the way; couldn't afford

another storeroom racket,' and soon the pine forest had swallowed up the stranger, his three led horses, and the two little bears.

'Well, I'm glad he's gone,' said Lan, savagely, though he knew quite well that he was already scourged with repentance. He began to set his shanty in order. He went to the storehouse and gathered the remnants of the provisions. After all, there was a good deal left. He walked past the box where Jack used to sleep. How silent it was! He noted the place where Jack used to scratch the door to get into the cabin, and started at the thought that he should hear it no more, and told himself, with many cuss-words, that he was 'mighty glad of it.' He pottered about, doing—doing—oh, anything, for an hour or more; then suddenly he leaped on his pony and raced madly down the trail on the track of the stranger. He put the pony hard to it, and in two hours he overtook the train at the crossing of the river.

'Say, pard, I done wrong. I didn't orter sell them little b'ars, leastwise not Jacky. I—I—wall, now, I want to call it off. Here's yer yellow.'

'I'm satisfied with my end of it,' said the stranger, coldly.

'Well, I ain't,' said Lan, with warmth, 'an' I want it off.'

'Ye're wastin' time if that's what ye come for,' was the reply.

'We'll see about that,' and Lan threw the gold pieces at the rider and walked over towards the pannier, where Jack was whining joyfully at the sound of the familiar voice.

'Hands up,' said the stranger, with the short, sharp tone of one who had said it before, and Lan turned to find himself covered with a .45 navy Colt.

'Ye got the drop on me,' he said; 'I ain't got no gun; but look-a here, stranger, that there little b'ar is the only pard I got; he's my stiddy company an' we're almighty fond o' each other. I didn't know how much I was a-goin' to miss him. Now look-a here: take back yer fifty; ye give me Jack an' keep Jill.'

'If ye got five hundred cold plunks in yaller ye kin get him; if not, you walk straight to that tree thar an' don't drop yer hands or turn or I'll fire. Now start.'

Mountain etiquette is very strict, and Lan, being without weapons, must needs obey the rules. He marched to the distant tree under cover of the revolver. The wail of little Jack smote painfully on his ear, but he knew the ways of the mountaineers too well to turn or make another offer, and the stranger went on.

Many a man has spent a thousand dollars in efforts to capture some wild thing and felt it worth the cost—for a time. Then he is willing to sell it for half cost, then for quarter, and at length he ends by giving it away. The stranger was vastly pleased with his comical bear cubs at first, and valued them proportionately; but each day they seemed more troublesome and less amusing, so that when, a week later, at the Bell-Cross Ranch, he was offered a horse for the pair, he readily closed, and their days of hamper-travel were over.

The owner of the ranch was neither mild, refined, nor patient. Jack, good-natured as he was, partly grasped these facts as he found himself taken from the pannier, but when it came to getting cranky little Jill out of the basket and into a collar, there ensued a scene so unpleasant that no collar was needed. The ranchman wore his hand in a sling for two weeks, and Jacky at his chain's end paced the ranch-yard alone.

The River held in the Foothills

THERE was little of pleasant interest in the next eighteen months of Jack's career. His share of the globe was a twenty-foot circle around a pole in the yard. The blue hills of the offing, the nearer pine grove, and even the ranch-house itself were fixed stars, far away and sending merely faint suggestions of their splendours to his not very bright eyes. Even the horses and men were outside his little sphere and related to him about as much as comets are to the earth. The very tricks that had made him valued were being forgotten as Jack grew up in chains.

At first a butter-firkin had made him an ample den, but he rapidly passed through the various stages—butter-firkin, nail-keg, flour-barrel, oil-barrel—and had now to be graded as a good average hogshead bear, though he was far from filling that big round wooden cavern that formed his latest den.

The ranch hotel lay just where the foothills of the Sierras with their groves of live oaks were sloping into the golden plains of the Sacramento. Nature had showered on it every wonderful gift in her lap. A foreground rich with flowers, luxuriant in fruit, shade and sun, dry pastures, rushing rivers,

and murmuring rills, were here. Great trees were variants of the view, and the high Sierras to the east overtopped the wondrous plumy forests of their pines with blocks of sculptured blue. Back of the house was a noble river of water from the hills, fouled and chained by sluice and dam, but still a noble stream whose earliest parent rill had gushed from grim old Tallac's slope.

Things of beauty, life, and colour were on every side, and yet most sordid of the human race were the folk about the ranch hotel. To see them in this setting might well raise doubt that any 'rise from Nature up to Nature's God.' No city slum has ever shown a more ignoble crew, and Jack, if his mind were capable of such things, must have graded the two-legged ones lower in proportion as he knew them better.

Cruelty was his lot, and hate was his response. Almost the only amusing trick he now did was helping himself to a drink of beer. He was very fond of beer, and the loafers about the tavern often gave him a bottle to see how dexterously he would twist off the wire and work out the cork. As soon as it popped, he would turn it up between his paws and drink to the last drop.

The monotony of his life was occasionally varied with a dog fight. His tormentors would bring their bear dogs 'to try them on the cub.' It seemed to be very pleasant sport to men and dogs, till Jack learned how to receive them. At first he used to rush furiously at the nearest tormentor until brought up with a jerk at the end of his chain and completely exposed to attack behind from another dog. A month or two entirely changed his method. He learned to sit against the hogshead and quietly watch the noisy dogs around him, with much show of inattention, making no move, no matter how near they were, until they 'bunched,' that is, gathered in one place. Then he charged. It was inevitable that the hind dogs would be the last to jump, and so hindered the front ones;

thus Jack would 'get' one or more of them, and the game became unpopular.

When about eighteen months old, and half grown, an incident took place which defied all explanation. Jack had won the name of being dangerous, for he had crippled one man with a blow and nearly killed a tipsy fool who volunteered to fight him. A harmless but good-for-nothing sheep-herder who loafed about the place got very drunk one night and offended some fire-eaters. They decided that, as he had no gun, it would be the proper thing to club him to their hearts' content instead of shooting him full of holes, in the manner usually prescribed by their code. Faco Tampico made for the door and staggered out into the darkness. His pursuers were even more drunk, but, bent on mischief, they gave chase, and Faco dodged back of the house and into the yard. The mountaineers had just wit enough to keep out of reach of the Grizzly as they searched about for their victim, but they did not find him. Then they got torches, and making sure that he was not in the yard, were satisfied that he had fallen into the river behind the barn and doubtless was drowned. A few rude jokes, and they returned to the house. As they passed the Grizzly's den their lanterns awoke in his eyes a glint of fire. In the morning the cook, beginning his day, heard strange sounds in the yard. They came from the Grizzly's den: 'Hyar, you, lay over dahr,' in sleepy tones; then a deep, querulous grunting.

The cook went as close as he dared and peeped in. Said the same voice in sleepy tones: 'Who are ye crowdin' caramba!' and a human elbow was seen jerking and pounding; and again impatient growling in bear-like tones was the response.

The sun came up and the astonished loafers found it was the missing sheep-herder that was in the bear's den, calmly sleeping off his debauch in the very cave of death. The men tried to get him out, but the Grizzly plainly showed that they

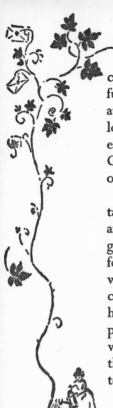

could do so only over his dead body. He charged with vindictive fury at any who ventured near, and when they gave up the attempt he lay down at the door of the den on guard. At length the sheep-herder came to himself, rose up on his elbows, and realizing that he was in the power of the young Grizzly, he stepped gingerly over his guardian's back and ran off without even saying 'Thank you.'

The Fourth of July was at hand now, and the owner of the tavern, growing weary of the huge captive in the yard, announced that he would celebrate Independence Day with a grand fight between a 'picked and fighting range bull and a ferocious Californian Grizzly.' The news was spread far and wide by the 'Grapevine Telegraph.' The roof of the stable was covered with seats at fifty cents each. The hay-wagon was half loaded and drawn alongside the corral; seats here gave a perfect view and were sold at a dollar apiece. The old corral was repaired, new posts put in where needed, and the first thing in the morning a vicious old bull was herded in and tormented till he was 'snuffy' and extremely dangerous.

Jack meanwhile had been roped, 'choked down,' and nailed up in his hogshead. His chain and collar were permanently riveted together, so the collar was taken off, as 'it would be easy to rope him, *if need be, after the bull was through with him.*'

The hogshead was rolled over to the corral gate and all was ready.

The cowboys came from far and near in their most gorgeous trappings, and the California cowboy is the peacock of his race. Their best girls were with them, and farmers and ranchmen came for fifty miles to enjoy the Bull-and-Bear fight. Miners from the hills were there, Mexican sheep-herders, storekeepers from Placerville, strangers from Sacramento; town and county, mountain and plain, were represented. The hay-wagon went so well that another was brought into market. The barn roof was sold out. An ominous crack of the timbers somewhat shook the prices, but a couple of strong uprights below restored the market, and all 'The Corners' was ready and eager for the great fight. Men who had been raised among cattle were betting on the bull.

'I tell you, there ain't nothing on earth kin face a big range bull that hez good use of hisself.'

But the hillmen were backing the bear. 'Pooh, what's a bull to a Grizzly? I tell you, I seen a Grizzly send a horse clean over the Hetch-Hetchy with one clip of his left. Bull! I'll bet he'll never show up in the second round.'

So they wrangled and bet, while burly women, trying to look fetching, gave themselves a variety of airs, were 'scared at the whole thing, nervous about the uproar, afraid it would be shocking,' but really were as keenly interested as the men.

All was ready, and the boss of 'The Corners' shouted: 'Let her go, boys; house is full an' time's up!'

Faco Tampico had managed to tie a bundle of chaparral thorn to the bull's tail, so that the huge creature had literally lashed himself into a frenzy.

Jack's hogshead meanwhile had been rolled around till he was raging with disgust, and Faco, at the word of command, began to pry open the door. The end of the barrel was close to the fence, the door cleared away; now there was nothing for Jack to do but to go forth and claw the bull to pieces. But he did not go. The noise, the uproar, the strangeness of the crowd affected him so that he decided to stay where he was, and the bull-backers raised a derisive cry. Their champion came forward bellowing and sniffing, pausing often to paw the dust. He held his head very high and approached slowly until he came within ten feet of the Grizzly's den; then giving a snort, he turned and ran to the other end of the corral. Now it was the bear-backers' turn to shout.

But the crowd wanted a fight, and Faco, forgetful of his debt to Grizzly Jack, dropped a bundle of Fourth of July crackers into the hogshead by way of the bung. 'Crack!' and Jack jumped up. '*Fizz—crack—c-r-r-a-a-c-k, cr-k-crk-ck!*' and Jack in surprise rushed from his den into the arena. The bull was standing in a magnificent attitude there in the middle, but when he saw the bear spring towards him, he gave two mighty snorts and retreated as far as he could, amid cheers and hisses.

Perhaps the two main characteristics of the Grizzly are the quickness with which he makes a plan and the vigour with which he follows it up. Before the bull had reached the far side of the corral Jack seemed to know the wisest of courses. His pig-like eyes swept the fence in a flash—took in the most climbable part, a place where a cross-piece was nailed on in the middle. In three seconds he was there, in two seconds he was over, and in one second he dashed through the running, scattering mob and was making for the hills as fast as his strong and supple legs could carry him. Women screamed, men yelled, and dogs barked; there was a wild dash for the horses tied far from the scene of the fight, to spare their nerves, but the Grizzly had three hundred yards' start, five hundred yards even, and before the gala mob gave out a long and flying column of reckless, riotous riders, the Grizzly had plunged into the river, a flood no dog cared to face, and had reached the chaparral and the broken ground in line for the piney hills. In an hour the ranch hotel, with its galling chain, its cruelties, and its brutal human beings, was a thing of the past, shut out by the hills of his youth, cut off by the river of his cubhood, the river grown from the rill born in his birthplace away in Tallac's pines. That Fourth of July was a glorious Fourth—it was Independence Day for Grizzly Jack.

6

The Broken Dam

A WOUNDED deer usually works downhill, a hunted Grizzly climbs. Jack knew nothing of the country, but he did know that he wanted to get away from that mob, so he sought the roughest ground, and climbed and climbed.

He had been alone for hours, travelling up and on. The plain was lost to view. He was among the granite rocks, the pine trees, and the berries now, and he gathered in food from the low bushes with dexterous paws and tongue as he travelled, but stopped not at all until among the tumbled rock, where the sun heat of the afternoon seemed to command rather than invite him to rest.

The night was black when he awoke, but bears are not afraid of the dark—they rather fear the day—and he swung along, led, as before, by the impulse to get up above the danger; and thus at last he reached the highest range, the region of his native Tallac.

He had but little of the usual training of a young bear, but all the main instincts, his birthright, that stood him well in all the main issues, and his nose was an excellent guide. Thus he managed to live, and wild-life experiences coming fast gave his mind the chance to grow.

Jack's memory for faces and facts was not at all good, but his memory for smells was imperishable. He had forgotten Bonamy's cur, but the smell of Bonamy's cur would instantly have thrilled him with the old feelings. He had forgotten the cross ram, but the smell of 'Old Woolly Whiskers' would have inspired him at once with anger and hate; and one evening when the wind came richly laden with ram smell it was like a bygone life returned. He had been living on roots and berries for weeks and now began to experience that hankering for flesh that comes on every candid vegetarian with dangerous force from time to time. The ram smell seemed an answer to it. So down he went by night (no sensible bear travels by day), and the smell brought him from the pines on the hillside to an open rocky dale.

Long before he got there a curious light shone up. He knew what that was; he had seen the two-legged ones make it near the ranch of evil smells and memories, so feared it not. He swung along from ledge to ledge in silence and in haste, for the smell of sheep grew stronger at every stride, and when he reached a place above the fire he blinked his eyes to find the sheep. The smell was strong now; it was rank, but no sheep to be seen. Instead he saw in the valley a stretch of grey water that seemed to reflect the stars, and yet they neither twinkled nor rippled; there was a murmuring sound from the sheet, but it seemed not at all like that of the lakes around.

The stars were clustered chiefly near the fire, and were less like stars than spots of the phosphorescent wood that are scattered on the ground when one knocks a rotten stump about to lick up its swarms of wood-ants. So Jack came closer, and at last so close that even his dull eyes could see. The great grey lake was a flock of sheep and the phosphorescent specks were their eyes. Close by the fire was a log or a low rough bank—that turned out to be the shepherd and his dog. Both were objectionable features, but the sheep extended far from them. Jack knew that his business was with the flock.

He came very close to the edge and found them surrounded by a low hedge of chaparral; but what little things they were compared with that great and terrible ram that he dimly remembered! The bloodthirst came on him. He swept the low hedge aside, charged into the mass of sheep that surged away from him with rushing sounds of feet and murmuring groans, struck down one, seized it, and turning away, he scrambled back up the mountains.

The sheep-herder leaped to his feet, fired his gun, and the dog came running over the solid mass of sheep, barking loudly. But Jack was gone. The sheep-herder contented himself with making two or three fires, shooting off his gun, and telling his beads.

That was Jack's first mutton, but it was not the last. Thenceforth when he wanted a sheep—and it became a regular need —he knew he had merely to walk along the ridge till his nose said, 'Turn, and go so,' for smelling is believing in bear life.

7

The Freshet

PEDRO TAMPICO and his brother Faco were not in the sheep business for any maudlin sentiment. They did not march ahead of their beloveds waving a crook as wand of office or appealing to the esthetic sides of their ideal followers with a tabret and pipe. Far from leading the flock with a symbol, they drove them with an armful of ever-ready rocks and clubs. They were not shepherds; they were sheep-herders. They did not view their charges as loved and loving followers, but as four-legged cash; each sheep was worth a dollar bill. They were cared for only as a man cares for his money, and counted after each alarm or day of travel. It is not easy for any one to count three thousand sheep, and for a Mexican sheep-herder it is an impossibility. But he has a simple device which answers the purpose. In an ordinary flock about one sheep in a hundred is a black one. If a portion of the flock has gone astray, there is likely to be a black one in it. So by counting his thirty black sheep each day Tampico kept rough count of his entire flock.

Grizzly Jack had killed but one sheep that first night. On his next visit he killed two, and on the next but one, yet that last one happened to be black, and when Tampico found but

twenty-nine of its kind remaining he safely reasoned that he was losing sheep—according to the index a hundred were gone.

'If the land is unhealthy move out' is ancient wisdom. Tampico filled his pocket with stones, and reviling his charges in all their walks in life and history, he drove them from the country that was evidently the range of a sheep-eater. At night he found a walled-in canyon, a natural corral, and the woolly scattering swarm, condensed into a solid fleece, went pouring into the gap, urged intelligently by the dog and idiotically by the man. At one side of the entrance Tampico made his fire. Some thirty feet away was a sheer wall of rock.

Ten miles may be a long day's travel for a wretched wool-plant, but it is little more than two hours for a Grizzly. It is farther than eyesight, but it is well within nosesight, and Jack, feeling mutton-hungry, had not the least difficulty in following his prey. His supper was a little later than usual, but his appetite was the better for that. There was no alarm in camp, so Tampico had fallen asleep. A growl from the dog awakened him. He started up to behold the most appalling creature that he had ever seen or imagined, a monster bear standing on his hind legs, and thirty feet high at least. The dog fled in terror, but was valour itself compared with Pedro. He was so frightened that he could not express the prayer that was in his breast: 'Blessed saints, let him have every sin-blackened sheep in the band, but spare your poor worshipper,' and he hid his head; so never learned that he saw, not a thirty-foot bear thirty feet away, but a seven-foot bear not far from the fire and casting a black thirty-foot shadow on the smooth rock behind. And helpless with fear, poor Pedro grovelled in the dust.

When he looked up the giant bear was gone. There was a rushing of the sheep. A small body of them scurried out of the canyon into the night, and after them went an ordinary-sized bear, undoubtedly a cub of the monster.

Pedro had been neglecting his prayers for some months back, but he afterward assured his father confessor that on this night he caught up on all arrears and had a goodly surplus before morning. At sunrise he left his dog in charge of the flock and set out to seek the runaways, knowing, first, that there was little danger in the daytime, second, that some would escape. The missing ones were a considerable number, raised to the second power indeed, for two more black ones were gone. Strange to tell, they had not scattered, and Pedro trailed them a mile or more in the wilderness till he reached another very small box canyon. Here he found the missing flock perched in various places on boulders and rocky pinnacles as high up as they could get. He was delighted and worked for half a minute on his bank surplus of prayers, but was sadly upset to find that nothing would induce the sheep to come down from the rocks or leave that canyon. One or two that he manœuvered as far as the outlet sprang back in fear from *something on the ground*, which, on examination, he found— yes, he swears to this—to be the deep-worn, fresh-worn pathway of a Grizzly from one wall across to the other. All the sheep were now back again beyond his reach. Pedro began to fear for himself, so hastily returned to the main flock. He was worse off than ever now. The other Grizzly was a bear of ordinary size and ate a sheep each night, but the new one, into whose range he had entered, was a monster, a bear mountain, requiring forty or fifty sheep to a meal. The sooner he was out of this the better.

It was now late, too late, and the sheep were too tired to travel, so Pedro made unusual preparations for the night: two big fires at the entrance to the canyon, and a platform fifteen feet up in a tree for his own bed. The dog could look out for himself.

. . . a monster bear . . . (*see page 25*)

8

Roaring in the Canyon

PEDRO knew that the big bear was coming; for the fifty
sheep in the little canyon were not more than an appetizer
for such a creature. He loaded his gun carefully as a matter of
habit and went upstairs to bed. Whatever defects his dormitory
had the ventilation was good, and Pedro was soon a-shiver. He
looked down in envy at his dog curled up by the fire; then he
prayed that the saints might intervene and direct the steps of
the bear towards the flock of some neighbour, and carefully
specified the neighbour to avoid mistakes. He tried to pray
himself to sleep. It had never failed in church when he was at
the Mission, so why now? But for once it did not succeed.
The fearsome hour of midnight passed, then the grey dawn,
the hour of dull despair, was near. Tampico felt it, and a long
groan vibrated through his chattering teeth. His dog leaped
up, barked savagely, the sheep began to stir, then went backing
into the gloom; there was a rushing of stampeding sheep and a
huge, dark form loomed up. Tampico grasped his gun and
would have fired, when it dawned on him with sickening
horror that the bear was thirty feet high, his platform was
only fifteen, just a convenient height for the monster. None

but a madman would invite the bear to eat by shooting at him now. So Pedro flattened himself face downward on the platform, and, with his mouth to a crack, he poured forth prayers to his representative in the sky, regretting his unconventional attitude and profoundly hoping that it would be overlooked as unavoidable, and that somehow the petitions would get the right direction after leaving the underside of the platform.

In the morning he had proof that his prayers had been favourably received. There was a bear-track, indeed, but the number of black sheep was unchanged, so Pedro filled his pocket with stones and began his usual torrent of remarks as he drove the flock.

'Hyah, Capitan—you huajalote,' as the dog paused to drink. 'Bring back those ill-descended sons of perdition,' and a stone gave force to the order, which the dog promptly obeyed. Hovering about the great host of grumbling hoofy locusts, he kept them together and on the move, while Pedro played the part of a big, noisy, and troublesome second.

As they journeyed through the open country the sheep-herder's eye fell on a human figure, a man sitting on a rock above them to the left. Pedro gazed inquiringly; the man saluted and beckoned. This meant 'friend'; had he motioned him to pass on it might have meant, 'Keep away or I shoot.' Pedro walked towards him a little way and sat down. The man came forward. It was Lan Kellyan, the hunter.

Each was glad of a chance to 'talk with a human' and to get the news. The latest concerning the price of wool, the bull-and-bear fiasco, and, above all, the monster bear, that had killed Tampico's sheep, afforded topics of talk. 'Ah, a bear devill—de hell-brute—a Gringo bear—pardon, my amigo, I mean a very terroar.'

As the sheep-herder enlarged on the marvellous

cunning of the bear that had a private sheep corral of his own, and the size of the monster, forty or fifty feet high now—for such bears are of rapid and continuous growth—Kellyan's eye twinkled and he said:

'Say, Pedro, I believe you once lived pretty nigh the Hassayampa, didn't you?'

This does not mean that that is a country of great bears, but was an allusion to the popular belief that any one who tastes a single drop of the Hassayampa River can never afterwards tell the truth. Some scientists who have looked into the matter aver that this wonderful property is common to the Rio Grande as well as the Hassayampa, and, indeed, all the rivers of Mexico, as well as their branches, and the springs, wells, ponds, lakes, and irrigation ditches. However that may be, the Hassayampa is the best-known stream of this remarkable peculiarity. The higher one goes, the greater its potency, and Pedro was from the head-waters. But he protested by all the saints that his story was true. He pulled out a little bottle of garnets, got by glancing over the rubbish laid about their hills by the desert ants; he thrust it back into his wallet and produced another bottle with a small quantity of gold-dust, also gathered at the rare times when he was not sleepy, and the sheep did not need driving, watering, stoning, or revilling.

'Here, I bet dat it ees so.'

Gold is a loud talker.

Kellyan paused. 'I can't cover your bet, Pedro, but I'll kill your bear for what's in the bottle.'

'I take you,' said the sheep-herder, 'eef you breeng back dose sheep dat are now starving up on de rocks of de canyon of Baxstaire's.'

The Mexican's eyes twinkled as the white man closed on the offer. The gold in the bottle, ten or fifteen dollars, was a trifle, and yet enough to send the hunter on the quest—enough to lure him into the enterprise, and that was all that was needed. Pedro knew his man: get him going and profit would count for nothing; having put his hand to the plough Lan Kellyan would finish the furrow at any cost; he was incapable of turning back. And again he took up the trail of Grizzly Jack, his one-time 'pard,' now grown beyond his ken.

The hunter went straight to Baxter's canyon and found the sheep high-perched upon the rocks. By the entrance he found the remains of two of them recently devoured, and about them the tracks of a medium-sized bear. He saw nothing of the pathway—the deadline—made by the Grizzly to keep the sheep prisoners till he should need them. But the sheep were standing in stupid terror on various high places, apparently willing to starve rather than come down.

Lan dragged one down; at once it climbed up again. He now realized the situation, so made a small pen of chaparral outside the canyon, and dragging the dull creatures down one at a time, he carried them—except one—out of the prison of death and into the pen. Next he made a hasty fence across the canyon's mouth, and turning the sheep out of the pen, he drove them by slow stages towards the rest of the flock.

Only six or seven miles across country, but it was late night when Lan arrived.

Tampico gladly turned over half of the promised dust. That night they camped together, and, of course, no bear appeared.

In the morning Lan went back to the canyon and found, as expected, that the bear had returned and killed the remaining sheep.

The hunter piled the rest of the carcasses in an open place, lightly sprinkled the Grizzly's trail with some very dry brush, then making a platform some fifteen feet from the ground in a tree, he rolled up in his blanket there and slept.

An old bear will rarely visit a place three nights in succession; a cunning bear will avoid a trail that has been changed overnight; a skilful bear goes in absolute silence. But Jack was neither old, cunning, nor skilful. He came for the fourth time to the canyon of the sheep. He followed his old trail straight to the delicious mutton bones. He found the human trail, but there was something about it that rather attracted him. He strode along on the dry boughs. '*Crack!*' went one; '*crack-crack!*' went another; and Kellyan arose on the platform and strained his eyes in the gloom till a dark form moved into the opening by the bones of the sheep. The hunter's rifle cracked, the bear snorted, wheeled into the bushes, and, crashing away, was gone.

9

Fire and Water

THAT was Jack's baptism of fire, for the rifle had cut a deep flesh-wound in his back. Snorting with pain and rage, he tore through the bushes and travelled on for an hour or more, then lay down and tried to lick the wound, but it was beyond reach. He could only rub it against a log. He continued his journey back towards Tallac, and there, in a cave that was formed of tumbled rocks, he lay down to rest. He was still rolling about in pain when the sun was high and a strange smell of fire came searching through the cave; it increased, and volumes of blinding smoke were about him. It grew so choking that he was forced to move, but it followed him till he could bear it no longer, and he dashed out of another of the ways that led into the cavern. As he went he caught a distant glimpse of a man throwing wood on the fire by the in-way, and the whiff that the wind brought him said: 'This is the man that was last night watching the sheep.' Strange as it may seem, the woods were clear of smoke except for a trifling belt that floated in the trees, and Jack went striding away in peace. He passed over the ridge, and finding berries, ate the first meal he had known since killing his last sheep. He had wandered

on, gathering fruit and digging roots, for an hour or two, when the smoke grew blacker, the smell of fire stronger. He worked away from it, but in no haste. The birds, deer, and wood hares were now seen scurrying past him. There was a roaring in the air. It grew louder, was coming nearer, and Jack turned to stride after the wood things that fled.

The whole forest was ablaze; the wind was rising, and the flames, gaining and spreading, were flying now like wild horses. Jack had no place in his brain for such a thing; but his instinct warned him to shun that coming roaring that sent above dark clouds and flying fire-flakes, and messengers of heat below, so he fled before it, as the forest host was doing. Fast as he went, and few animals can outrun a Grizzly in rough country, the hot hurricane was gaining on him. His sense of danger had grown almost to terror, terror of a kind that he had never known before, for here there was nothing he could fight; nothing that he could resist. The flames were all around him now; birds without number, hares, and deer had gone down before the red horror. He was plunging wildly on through chaparral and manzanita thickets that held all feebler things until the fury seized them; his hair was scorching, his wound was forgotten, and he thought only of escape when the brush ahead opened, and the Grizzly, smoke-blinded, half roasted, plunged down a bank and into a small clear pool. The fur on his back said 'hiss,' for it was sizzling-hot. Down below he went, gulping the cool drink, wallowing in safety and unheat. Down below the surface he crouched as long as his lungs would bear the strain, then slowly and cautiously he raised his head. The sky above was one great sheet of flame. Sticks aflame and flying embers came in hissing showers on the water. The air was hot, but breathable at times, and he filled his lungs till he had difficulty in keeping his body down below. Other creatures there were in the pool, some burnt, some dead, some small and in the margin, some bigger in the deeper

places, and one of them was close beside him. Oh, he knew
that smell; fire—all Sierra's woods ablaze—could not dis-
guise the hunter who had shot at him from the platform,
and, though he did not know this, the hunter really who had
followed him all day, and who had tried to smoke him out of
his den and thereby set the woods ablaze.

Here they were, face to face, in the deepest end of the
little pool; they were only ten feet apart and could not get
more than twenty feet apart. The flames grew unbearable.
The bear and man each took a hasty breath and bobbed below
the surface, each wondering, according to his intelligence,
what the other would do. In half a minute both came up again,
each relieved to find the other no nearer. Each tried to
keep his nose and one eye above the water. But the fire
was raging hot; they had to dip under and stay as long as
possible.

The roaring of the flame was like a hurricane. A huge pine
tree came crashing down across the pool; it barely missed the
man. The splash of water quenched the blazes for the most
part, but it gave off such a heat that he had to move—a little
nearer to the bear. Another fell at an angle, killing a coyote,
and crossing the first tree. They blazed fiercely at their junction,
and the bear edged from it a little nearer the man. Now they
were within touching distance. His useless gun was lying in
shallow water near shore, but the man had his knife ready,
ready for self-defence. It was not needed; the fiery power had
proclaimed a peace. Bobbing up and dodging under, keeping
a nose in the air and an eye on his foe, each spent an hour or
more. The red hurricane passed on. The smoke was bad in the
woods, but no longer intolerable, and as the bear straightened
up in the pool to move away into shallower water and off into
the woods, the man got a glimpse of red blood streaming from
the shaggy back and dyeing the pool. The blood on the trail
had not escaped him. He knew that this was the bear of

Baxter's canyon, this was the Gringo bear, but he did not know that this was also his old-time Grizzly Jack. He scrambled out of the pond, on the other side from that taken by the Grizzly, and, hunter and hunted, they went their diverse ways.

10

The Eddy

ALL the west slopes of Tallac were swept by the fire, and Kellyan moved to a new hut on the east side, where still were green patches; so did the grouse and the rabbit and the coyote, and so did Grizzly Jack. His wound healed quickly, but his memory of the rifle smell continued; it was a dangerous smell, a new and horrible kind of smoke—one he was destined to know too well; one, indeed, he was soon to meet again. Jack was wandering down the side of Tallac, following a sweet odour that called up memories of former joys—the smell of honey, though he did not know it. A flock of grouse got leisurely out of his way and flew to a low tree, when he caught a whiff of man smell, then heard a crack like that which had stung him in the sheep-corral, and down fell one of the grouse close beside him. He stepped forward to sniff just as a man also stepped forward from the opposite bushes. They were within ten feet of each other, and they recognized each other, for the hunter saw that it was a singed bear with a wounded side, and the bear smelt the rifle-smoke and the leather clothes. Quick as a Grizzly—that is, quicker than a flash—the bear reared. The man sprang backwards, tripped and

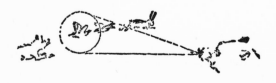

fell, and the Grizzly was upon him. Face to earth the hunter lay like dead, but, ere he struck, Jack caught a scent that made him pause. He smelt his victim, and the smell was the rolling back of curtains or the conjuring up of a past. The days in the hunter's shanty were forgotten, but the feeling of those days were ready to take command at the bidding of the nose. His nose drank deep of a draft that quelled all rage. The Grizzly's humour changed. He turned and left the hunter quite unharmed.

Oh, blind one with the gun! All he could find in explanation was: 'You kin never tell what a Grizzly will do, but it's good play to lay low when he has you cornered.' It never came into his mind to credit the shaggy brute with an impulse born of good, and when he told the sheep-herder of his adventure in the pool, of his hitting high on the body and of losing the trail in the forest fire—'down by the shack, when he turned up sudden and had me I thought my last day was come. Why he didn't swat me, I don't know. But I tell you this, Pedro: the b'ar what killed your sheep on the upper pasture and in the sheep canyon is the same. No two b'ars has hind feet alike when you get a clear-cut track, and this holds out even right along.'

'What about the fifty-foot b'ar I saw wit' mine own eyes, caramba?'

'That must have been the night you were working a kill-care with your sheep-herder's delight. But don't worry; I'll get him yet.'

So Kellyan set out on a long hunt, and put in practice every trick he knew for the circumventing of a bear. Lou Bonamy was invited to join with him, for his yellow cur was a trailer. They packed four horses with stuff and led them over the ridge to the east side of Tallac, and down away from Jack's Peak, that Kellyan had named in honour of his bear cub, towards Fallen Leaf Lake. The hunter believed that here he would meet not only the Gringo bear that he was after, but would

also stand a chance of finding others, for the place had escaped the fire.

They quickly camped, setting up their canvas sheet for shade more than against rain, and, after picketing their horses in a meadow, went out to hunt. By circling around Leaf Lake they got a good idea of the wild population: plenty of deer, some Black bear, and one or two Cinnamon and Grizzly, and one track along the shore that Kellyan pointed to, briefly saying: 'That's him.'

'Ye mean old Pedro's Gringo?'

'Yep. That's the fifty-foot Grizzly. I suppose he stands maybe seven foot high in daylight, but, 'course, b'ars pulls out long at night.'

So the yellow cur was put on the track, and led away with funny little yelps, while the two hunters came stumbling along behind him as fast as they could, calling, at times, to the dog not to go so fast, and thus making a good deal of noise, which Gringo Jack heard a mile away as he ambled along the mountainside above them. He was following his nose to many good and eatable things, and therefore going up-wind. This noise behind was so peculiar that he wanted to smell it, and to do that he swung along back over the clamour, then descended to the down-wind side, and thus he came on the trail of the hunters and their dog.

His nose informed him at once. Here was the hunter he once felt kindly towards and two other smells of far-back—both hateful; all three were now the smell-marks of foes, and a rumbling '*woof*' was the expressive sound that came from his throat.

That dog-smell in particular roused him, though it is very sure he had forgotten all about the dog, and Gringo's feet went swiftly and silently, yes, with marvellous silence, along the tracks of the enemy.

On rough, rocky ground a dog is scarcely quicker than a

bear, and since the dog was constantly held back by the hunters the bear had no difficulty in overtaking them. Only a hundred yards or so behind he continued, partly in curiosity, pursuing the dog that was pursuing him, till a shift of the wind brought the dog a smell-call from the bear behind. He wheeled—of course you never follow trail smell when you can find body smell—and came galloping back with a different yapping and a bristling in his mane.

'Don't understand that,' whispered Bonamy.

'It's b'ar, all right,' was the answer; and the dog, bounding high, went straight towards the foe.

Jack heard him coming, smelt him coming, and at length saw him coming; but it was the smell that roused him—the full scent of the bully of his youth. The anger of those days came on him, and cunning enough to make him lurk in ambush: he backed to one side of the trail where it passed under a root, and, as the little yellow tyrant came, Jack hit him once, hit him as he had done some years before, but now with the power of a grown Grizzly. No yelp escaped the dog, no second blow was needed. The hunters searched in silence for half an hour before they found the place and learned the tale from many silent tongues.

'I'll get even with him,' muttered Bonamy, for he loved that contemptible little yap-cur.

'That's Pedro's Gringo, all right. He's sure cunning to run his own back track. But we'll fix him yet,' and they vowed to kill that bear or 'get done up' themselves.

Without a dog, they must make a new plan of hunting. They picked out two or three good places for pen-traps, where trees stood in pairs to make the pillars of the den. Then Kellyan returned to camp for the axe while Bonamy prepared the ground.

As Kellyan came near their open camping-place, he stopped from habit and peeped ahead for a minute. He was about to go down when a movement caught his eye. There, on his haunches, sat a Grizzly, looking down on the camp. The singed brown of his head and neck, and the white spot on each side of his back, left no doubt that Kellyan and Pedro's Gringo were again face to face. It was a long shot, but the rifle went up, and as he was about to fire, the bear suddenly bent his head down, and lifting his hind paw, began to lick at a little cut. This brought the head and chest nearly in line with Kellyan—a sure shot; so sure that he fired hastily. He missed the head and the shoulder, but, strange to say, he hit the bear in the mouth and in the hind toe, carrying away one of his teeth and the side of one toe. The Grizzly sprang up with a snort, and came tearing down the hill towards the hunter. Kellyan climbed a tree and got ready, but the camp lay just between them, and the bear charged on that instead. One sweep of his paw and the canvas tent was down and torn. Whack! and tins went flying this way. Whisk! and flour-sacks went that. Rip! and the flour went off like smoke. Slap—crack! and a boxful of odds and ends was scattered into the fire. Whack! and a bagful of cartridges was tumbled after it. Whang! and the water-pail was crushed. Pat-pat-pat! and all the cups were in useless bits.

Kellyan, safe up the tree, got no fair view to shoot—could only wait till the storm-centre cleared a little. The bear chanced on a bottle of something with a cork loosely in it. He seized it adroitly in his paws, twisted out the cork, and held the bottle up to his mouth with a comical dexterity that told of previous experience. But, whatever it was, it did not please the invader; he spat and spilled it out, and flung the bottle down as Kellyan gazed, astonished. A remarkable *crack! crack! crack!* from the fire was heard now, and the cartridges began to go off in ones, twos, fours, and numbers unknown. Gringo whirled about; he had smashed everything in view. He did not like that Fourth of July sound, so, springing to a bank, he went bumping and heaving down to the meadow and

had just stampeded the horses when, for the first time, Gringo exposed himself to the hunter's aim. His flank was grazed by another leaden stinger, and Gringo, wheeling, went off into the woods.

The hunters were badly defeated. It was fully a week before they had repaired all the damage done by their shaggy visitor and were once more at Fallen Leaf Lake with a new store of ammunition and provisions, their tent repaired, and their camp outfit complete. They said little about their vow to kill that bear. Both took for granted that it was a fight to the finish. They never said, '*If* we get him,' but, '*When* we get him.'

11

The Ford

GRINGO, savage, but still discreet, scaled the long mountainside when he left the ruined camp, and afar on the southern slope he sought a quiet bed in a manzanita thicket, there to lie down and nurse his wounds and ease his head so sorely aching with the jar of his shattered tooth. There he lay for a day and a night, sometimes in great pain, and at no time inclined to stir. But, driven forth by hunger on the second day, he quit his couch and, making for the nearest ridge, he followed that and searched the wind with his nose. The smell of a mountain hunter reached him. Not knowing just what to do he sat down and did nothing. The smell grew stronger, he heard sounds of trampling; closer they came, then the brush parted and a man on horseback appeared. The horse snorted and tried to wheel, but the ridge was narrow and one false step might have been serious. The cowboy held his horse in hand and, although he had a gun, he made no attempt to shoot at the surly animal blinking at him and barring his path. He was an old mountaineer, and he now used a trick that had long been practised by the Indians, from whom, indeed, he learned it. He began 'making medicine with his voice.'

'See here now, B'ar,' he called aloud, 'I ain't doing nothing to you. I ain't got no grudge ag'in' you, an' you ain't got no right to a grudge ag'in' me.'

'*Gro-o-o-h*,' said Gringo, deep and low.

'Now, I don't want no scrap with you, though I have my scrap-iron right handy, an' what I want you to do is just step aside an' let me pass that narrer trail an' go about my business.'

'*Grow-woo-oo-wow*,' grumbled Gringo.

'I'm honest about it, pard. You let me alone, and I'll let you alone; all I want is right of way for five minutes.'

'*Grow-grow-wow-oo-umph*,' was the answer.

'Ye see, thar's no way round an' on'y one way through, an' you happen to be settin' in it. I got to take it, for I can't turn back. Come, now, is it a bargain—hands off and no scrap?'

It is very sure that Gringo could see in this nothing but a human making queer, unmenacing, monotonous sounds, so giving a final '*Gr-u-ph*,' the bear blinked his eyes, rose to his feet and strode down the bank, and the cowboy forced his unwilling horse to and past the place.

'Wall, wall,' he chuckled, 'I never knowed it to fail. Thar's whar most b'ars is alike.'

If Gringo had been able to think clearly, he might have said: 'This surely is a new kind of man.'

12

Swirl and Pool and Growing Flood

GRINGO wandered on with nose alert, passing countless odours of berries, roots, grouse, deer, till a new and pleasing smell came with especial force.

It was not sheep, or game, or a dead thing. It was a smell of living meat. He followed the guide to a little meadow and there he found it. There were five of them, red, or red and white—great things as big as himself; but he had no fear of them. The hunter instinct came on him, and the hunter's audacity and love of achievement. He sneaked towards them upwind in order that he might still smell them, and it also kept them from smelling him. He reached the edge of the wood. Here he must stop or be seen. There was a watering-place close by. He silently drank, then lay down in a thicket where he could watch. An hour passed thus. The sun went down and the cattle arose to graze. One of them, a small one, wandered nearer, then, acting suddenly with purpose, walked to the water-hole. Gringo watched his chance, and as she floundered in the mud and stooped he reared and struck with all his force. Square at her skull he aimed, and the blow went straight. But Gringo knew nothing of horns. The young,

sharp horn, upcurling, hit his foot and was broken off; the blow lost half its power. The beef went down, but Gringo had to follow up the blow, then raged and tore in anger for his wounded paw. The other cattle fled from the scene. The Grizzly took the heifer in his jaws, then climbed the hill to his lair, and with this store of food he again lay down to nurse his wounds. Though painful, they were not serious, and within a week or so Grizzly Jack was as well as ever and roaming the woods about Fallen Leaf Lake and farther south and east, for he was extending his range as he grew—the king was coming to his kindgom. In time he met others of his kind and matched his strength with theirs. Sometimes he won and sometimes lost, but he kept on growing as the months went by, growing and learning and adding to his power.

Kellyan had kept track of him and knew at least the main facts of his life, because he had one or two marks that always served to distinguish him. A study of the tracks had told of the round wound in the front foot and the wound in the hind foot. But there was another: the hunter had picked up the splinters of bone at the camp where he had fired at the bear, and, after long doubt, he guessed that he had broken a tusk. He hesitated to tell the story of hitting a tooth and hind toe at the same shot till, later, he had clearer proof of its truth.

No two animals are alike. Kinds which herd have more sameness than those that do not, and the Grizzly, being a solitary kind, shows great individuality. Most Grizzlies mark their length on the trees by rubbing their backs, and some will turn on the tree and claw it with their forepaws; others hug the tree with forepaws and rake it with their hind claws. Gringo's peculiarity of marking was to rub first, then turn and tear the trunk with his teeth.

It was on examining one of the bear trees one day that Kellyan discovered the facts. He had been

tracking the bear all morning, had a fine set of tracks in the dusty trail, and thus learned that the rifle-wound was a toe-shot in the hind foot, but his fore foot of the same side had a large round wound, the one really made by the cow's horn. When he came to the bear tree where Gringo had carved his initials, the marks were clearly made by the bear's teeth, and one of the upper tusks was broken off, so the evidence of identity was complete.

'It's the same old b'ar,' said Lan to his pard.

They failed to get sight of him in all this time, so the partners set to work at a series of bear-traps. These are made of heavy logs and have a sliding door of hewn planks. The bait is on a trigger at the far end; a tug on this lets the door drop. It was a week's hard work to make four of these traps. They did not set them at once, for no bear will go near a thing so suspiciously new-looking. Some bears will not approach one till it is weather-beaten and grey. But they removed all chips and covered the newly cut wood with mud, then rubbed the inside with stale meat, and hung a lump of ancient venison on the trigger of each trap.

They did not go around for three days, knowing that the human smell must first be dissipated, and then they found but one trap sprung—the door down. Bonamy became greatly excited, for they had crossed the Grizzly's track close by. But Kellyan had been studying the dust and suddenly laughed aloud.

'Look at that,'—he pointed to a thing like a bear-track, but scarcely two inches long. 'There's the b'ar we'll find in that; that's a bushy-tailed b'ar,' and Bonamy joined in the laugh when he realized that the victim in the big trap was nothing but a little skunk.

'Next time we'll set the bait higher and not set the trigger so fine.'

They rubbed their boots with stale meat when they went the rounds, then left the traps for a week.

There are bears that eat little but roots and berries; there are bears that love best the great black salmon they can hook out of the pools when the long 'run' is on; and there are bears that have a special fondness for flesh. These are rare; they are apt to develop unusual ferocity and meet an early death. Gringo was one of them, and he grew like the brawny, meat-fed gladiators of old—bigger, stronger, and fiercer than his fruit- and root-fed kin. In contrast with this was his love of honey. The hunter on his trail learned that he never failed to dig out any bees' nest he could find, or, finding none, he would eat the little honey-flowers that hung like sleigh-bells on the heather. Kellyan was quick to mark the signs. 'Say, Bonamy, we've got to find some honey.'

It is not easy to find a bee tree without honey to fill your bee-guides; so Bonamy rode down the mountain to the nearest camp, the Tampico sheep camp, and got not honey but some sugar, of which they made syrup. They caught bees at three or four different places, tagged them with cotton, filled them with syrup and let them fly, watching till the cotton tufts were lost to view, and by going on the lines till they met they found the hive. A piece of gunny-sack filled with comb was put on each trigger, and that night, as Gringo strode with that long, untiring swing that eats up miles like stream-wheels, his sentinel nose reported the delicious smell, the one that above the rest meant joy. So Gringo Jack followed fast and far, for the place was a mile away, and reaching the curious log cavern, he halted and sniffed. There were hunters' smells; yes, but, above all, that smell of joy. He walked around to be sure, and knew it was inside; then cautiously he entered. Some wood-mice scurried by. He sniffed the bait, licked it, mumbled it, slobbered it, revelled in it, tugged to increase the flow, when '*bang!*' went the great door behind and Jack was caught. He

backed up with a rush, bumped into the door, and had a sense, at least, of peril. He turned over with an effort and attacked the door, but it was strong. He examined the pen; went all around the logs where their rounded sides seemed easiest to tear at with his teeth. But they yielded nothing. He tried them all; he tore at the roof, the floor; but all were heavy, hard logs, spiked and pinned as one.

The sun came up as he raged, and shone through the little cracks of the door, and so he turned all his power on that. The door was flat, gave little hold, but he battered with his paws and tore with his teeth till plank after plank gave way. With a final crash he drove the wreck before him and Jack was free again.

The men read the story as though in print; yes, better, for bits of plank can tell no lies, and the track to the pen and from the pen was the track of a big bear with a cut on the hind foot and a curious round peg-like scar on the front paw, while the logs inside, where little torn, gave proof of a broken tooth.

'We had him that time, but he knew too much for us. Never mind, we'll see.'

So they kept on and caught him again, for honey he could not resist. But the wreckage of the trap was all they found in the morning.

Pedro's brother knew a man who had trapped bears, and the sheep-herder remembered that it is necessary to have the door quite *light-tight* rather than very strong, so they battened all with tar-paper outside. But Gringo was learning 'pen-traps.' He did not break the door that he did not see through, but he put one paw under and heaved it up when he had finished the bait. Thus he baffled them and sported with the traps, till Kellyan made the door drop into a deep groove so that the bear could put no claw beneath it. But it was cold weather now. There was deepening snow on the Sierras. The bear sign disappeared. The hunters knew that Gringo was sleeping his winter's sleep.

13

The Deepening Channel

APRIL was bidding high Sierra snows go back to Mother Sea. The California woodwales screamed in clamorous joy. They thought it was about a few acorns left in storage in the Live Oak bark, but it really was joy of being alive. This outcry was to them what music is to the thrush, what joy-bells are to us—a great noise to tell how glad they were. The deer were bounding, grouse were booming, rills were rushing—all things were full of noisy gladness.

Kellyan and Bonamy were back on the Grizzly quest. 'Time he was out again, and good trailing to get him, with lots of snow in the hollows.' They had come prepared for a long hunt. Honey for bait, great steel traps with crocodilian jaws, and guns there were in the outfit. The pen-trap, the better for the aging, was repaired and rebaited, and several Black bears were taken. But Gringo, if about, had learned to shun it.

He was about, and the men soon learned that. His winter sleep was over. They found the peg-print in the snow, but with it, or just ahead, was another, the tracks of a smaller bear.

'See that,' and Kellyan pointed to the smaller mark. 'This is mating-time; this is Gringo's honeymoon,' and he followed

the trail for a while, not expecting to find them, but simply to know their movements. He followed several times and for miles, and the trail told him many things. Here was the track of a third bear joining. Here were marks of a combat, and a rival driven away was written there, and then the pair went on. Down from the rugged hills it took him once to where a love-feast had been set by the bigger bear; for the carcass of a steer lay half devoured, and the telltale ground said much of the struggle that foreran the feast. As though to show his power, the bear had seized the steer by the nose and held him for a while—so said the trampled earth for rods—struggling, bellowing, no doubt, music for my lady's ears, till Gringo judged it time to strike him down with paws of steel.

Once only the hunters saw the pair—a momentary glimpse of a bear so huge they half believed Tampico's tale, and a bear of lesser size in fur that rolled and rippled in the sun with brown and silver lights.

'Oh, ain't that just the beautifulest thing that ever walked!' and both the hunters gazed as she strode from view in the chaparral. It was only a neck of the thicket; they both must reappear in a minute at the other side, and the men prepared to fire; but for some incomprehensible reason the two did not appear again. They never quit the cover, and had wandered far away before the hunters knew it, and were seen of them no more.

But Faco Tampico saw them. He was visiting his brother with the sheep, and hunting in the foot-hills to the eastward, in hopes of getting a deer, his small black eyes fell on a pair of bears, still love-bound, roaming in the woods. They were far below him. He was safe, and he sent a ball that laid the she-bear low; her back was broken. She fell with a cry of pain and vainly tried to rise. Then Gringo rushed around, sniffed the wind for the foe, and Faco fired again. The sound and the smoke-puff told Gringo where the man lay hid. He

raged up the cliff, but Faco climbed a tree, and Gringo went
back to his mate. Faco fired again; Gringo made still another
effort to reach him, but could not find him now, so returned
to his 'Silver-brown.'

Whether it was chance or choice can never be known, but
when Faco fired once more, Gringo Jack was between, and
the ball struck him. It was the last in Faco's pouch, and the
Grizzly, charging as before, found not a trace of the foe. He
was gone—had swung across a place no bear could cross and
soon was a mile away. The big bear limped back to his mate,
but she no longer responded to his touch. He watched about
for a time, but no one came. The silver hide was never
touched by man, and when the semblance of his mate was
gone, Gringo quit the place.

The world was full of hunters, traps, and guns. He turned
towards the lower hills where the sheep grazed, where once
he had raided Pedro's flocks, limping along, for now he had
another flesh-wound. He found the scent of the foe that killed
his 'Silver-brown,' and would have followed, but it ceased
at a place where a horse-track joined. Yet he found it again
that night, mixed with the sheep smell so familiar once. He
followed this, sore and savage. It led him to a settler's flimsy
shack, the house of Tampico's parents, and as the big bear
reached it two human beings scrambled out of the rear door.

'My husband,' shrieked the woman, 'pray! Let us pray to
the saints for help!'

'Where is my pistol?' cried the husband.

'Trust in the saints,' said the frightened woman.

'Yes, if I had a cannon, or if this was a cat; but with only a
pepper-box pistol to meet a bear mountain it is better to trust
to a tree,' and old Tampico scrambled up a pine.

The Grizzly looked into the shack, then passed to the pig-
pen, killed the largest there, for this was a new kind of meat,
and carrying it off, he made his evening meal.

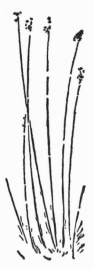

He came again and again to that pig-pen. He found his food there till his wound was healed. Once he met with a spring-gun, but it was set too high. Six feet up, the sheep-folk judged, would be just about right for such a bear; the charge went over his head, and so he passed unharmed—a clear proof that he was a devil. He was learning this: the human smell in any form is a smell of danger. He quit the little valley of the shack, wandering downward towards the plains. He passed a house one night, and walking up, he discovered a hollow thing with a delicious smell. It was a ten-gallon keg that had been used for sugar, some of which was still in the bottom, and thrusting in his huge head, the keg-rim, bristling with nails, stuck to him. He raged about, clawing at it wildly and roaring in it until a charge of shot from the upper windows stirred him to such effort that the keg was smashed to bits and his blinders removed.

Thus the idea was slowly borne in on him: going near a man-den is sure to bring trouble. Thenceforth he sought his prey in the woods or on the plains. He one day found the man scent that enraged him the day he lost his 'Silver-brown.' He took the trail, and passing in silence incredible for such a bulk, he threaded chaparral and manzanita on and down through tulé-beds till the level plain was reached. The scent led on, was fresher now. Far out were white specks—moving things. They meant nothing to Gringo, for he had never smelt wild geese, had scarcely seen them, but the trail he was hunting went on. He swiftly followed till the tulé ahead rustled gently, and the scent was *body scent*. A ponderous rush, a single blow— and the goose-hunt was ended ere well begun, and Faco's sheep became the brother's heritage.

14

The Foaming Flood

JUST as fads will for a time sway human life, so crazes may run through all animals of a given kind. This was the year when a beef-eating craze seemed to possess every able-bodied Grizzly of the Sierras. They had long been known as a root-eating, berry-picking, inoffensive race when let alone, but now they seemed to descend on the cattle-range in a body and make their diet wholly of flesh.

One cattle outfit after another was attacked, and the whole country seemed divided up among bears of incredible size, cunning, and destructiveness. The cattlemen offered bounties —good bounties, growing bounties, very large bounties at last—but still the bears kept on. Very few were killed, and it became a kind of rude jest to call each section of the range, not by the cattle brand, but by the Grizzly that was quartered on its stock.

Wonderful tales were told of these various bears of the new breed. The swiftest was Reelfoot, the Placerville cattle-killer that could charge from a thicket thirty yards away and certainly catch a steer before it could turn and run, and that could even catch ponies in the open when they were poor. The most

cunning of all was Brin, the Mokelumne Grizzly that killed by preference blooded stock, would pick out a Merino ram or a white-faced Hereford from among fifty grades; that killed a new beef every night; that never again returned to it, or gave the chance for traps or poisoning.

The Pegtrack Grizzly of Feather River was rarely seen by any. He was enveloped in mysterious terror. He moved and killed by night. Pigs were his favourite food, and he had also killed a number of men.

But Pedro's Grizzly was the most marvellous. 'Hassayampa,' as the sheep-herder was dubbed, came one night to Kellyan's hut.

'I tell you he's still dere. He has keel me a t'ousand sheep. You telled me you keel heem; you haff not. He is beegare as dat tree. He eat only sheep—much sheep. I tell you he ees Gringo devil—he ees devil bear. I haff three cows, two fat, one theen. He catch and keel de fat; de lean run off. He roll een dust—make great dust. Cow come for see what make dust; he catch her an' keel. My fader got bees. De devil bear chaw pine; I know he by hees broke toof. He gum hees face and nose wit' pine gum so bees no sting, then eat all bees. He devil all time. He get much rotten manzanita and eat till drunk—locoed—then go crazy and keel sheep just for fun. He get beeg bull by nose and drag like rat for fun. He keel cow, sheep, and keel Faco, too, for fun. He devil. You promise me you keel heem; you nevaire keel.'

This is a condensation of Pedro's excited account.

And there was yet one more—the big bear that owned the range from the Stanislaus to the Merced, the 'Monarch of the Range' he had been styled. He was believed—yes, known to be—the biggest bear alive, a creature of supernatural intelligence. He killed cows for food, and scattered sheep or conquered bulls for pleasure. It was even said that the appearance of an unusually big bull anywhere was a guarantee that Monarch

would be there for the joy of combat with a worthy foe. A destroyer of cattle, sheep, pigs, and horses, and yet a creature known only by his track. He was never seen, and his nightly raids seemed planned with consummate skill to avoid all kinds of snares.

The cattlemen clubbed together and offered an enormous bounty for every Grizzly killed in the range. Bear-trappers came and caught some bears, Brown and Cinnamon, but the cattle-killing went on. They set out better traps of massive steel and iron bars, and at length they caught a killer, the Mokelumne Grizzly; yes, and read in the dust how he had come at last and made the fateful step; but steel will break and iron will bend. The great bear-trail was there to tell the tale: for a while he had raged and chafed at the hard black reptile biting into his paw; then, seeking a boulder, he had released the paw by smashing the trap to pieces on it. Thenceforth each year he grew more cunning, huge, and destructive.

Kellyan and Bonamy came down from the mountains now, tempted by the offered rewards. They saw the huge tracks; they learned that cattle were not killed in all places at once. They studied and hunted. They got at length in the dust the full impressions of the feet of the various monsters in regions wide apart, and they saw that all the cattle were killed in the same way—their muzzles torn, their necks broken; and last, the marks on the trees where the bears had reared and rubbed, then scored them with a broken tusk, the same all through the wide range; and Kellyan told them with calm certainty: 'Pedro's Gringo, Old Pegtrack, the Placerville Grizzly, and the Monarch of the Range *are one and the same bear*.'

The little man from the mountains and the big man from the hills set about the task of hunting him down with an intensity of purpose which, like the river that is dammed, grew more fierce from being balked.

All manner of traps had failed for him. Steel traps he could

smash, no log trap was strong enough to hold this furry elephant; he would not come to a bait; he never fed twice from the same kill.

Two reckless boys once trailed him to a rocky glen. The horses would not enter; the boys went in afoot, and were never seen again. The Mexicans held him in superstitious terror, believing that he could not be killed; and he passed another year in the cattle-land, known and feared now as the 'Monarch of the Range,' killing in the open by night, and retiring by day to his fastness in the near hills, where horsemen could not follow.

Bonamy had been called away; but all that summer, and winter, too—for the Grizzly no longer 'denned up'—Kellyan rode and rode, each time too late or too soon to meet the Monarch. He was almost giving up, not in despair, but for lack of means, when a message came from a rich man, a city journalist, offering to multiply the reward by ten if, instead of killing the Monarch, he would bring him in alive.

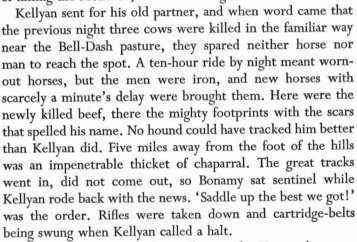

Kellyan sent for his old partner, and when word came that the previous night three cows were killed in the familiar way near the Bell-Dash pasture, they spared neither horse nor man to reach the spot. A ten-hour ride by night meant worn-out horses, but the men were iron, and new horses with scarcely a minute's delay were brought them. Here were the newly killed beef, there the mighty footprints with the scars that spelled his name. No hound could have tracked him better than Kellyan did. Five miles away from the foot of the hills was an impenetrable thicket of chaparral. The great tracks went in, did not come out, so Bonamy sat sentinel while Kellyan rode back with the news. 'Saddle up the best we got!' was the order. Rifles were taken down and cartridge-belts being swung when Kellyan called a halt.

'Say, boys, we've got him safe enough. He won't try to leave the chaparral till night. If we shoot him we get the cattlemen's bounty; if we take him alive—an' it's easy in the open—we get the newspaper bounty, ten times as big. Let's leave all guns behind; lariats are enough.'

'Why not have the guns along to be handy?'

''Cause I know the crowd too well; they couldn't resist the chance to let him have it; so no guns at all. It's ten to one on the riata.'

Nevertheless three of them brought their heavy revolvers. Seven gallant riders on seven fine horses, they rode out that day to meet the Monarch of the Range. He was still in the thicket, for it was yet morning. They threw stones in and shouted to drive him out, without effect, till the noon breeze of the plains arose—the down-current of air from the hills. Then they fired the grass in several places, and it sent a rolling sheet of flame and smoke into the thicket. There was a crackling louder than the fire, a smashing of brush, and from the farther side out hurled the Monarch bear, the Gringo, Grizzly Jack. Horsemen were all about him now, armed not with guns but with the rawhide snakes whose loops in air spell bonds or death. The men were calm, but the horses were snorting and plunging in fear. This way and that the Grizzly looked up at the horsemen—a little bit; scarcely up at the horses; then turning without haste, he strode towards the friendly hills.

'Look out, now, Bill! Manuel! It's up to you.'

Oh, noble horses, nervy men! Oh, grand old Grizzly, how I see you now! Cattle-keepers and cattle-killer face to face!

Three riders of the range that horse had never thrown were sailing, swooping, like falcons; their lariats swung, sang—sang higher—and Monarch, much perplexed, but scarcely angered yet, rose to his hind legs, then from his towering height looked down on horse and man. If, as they say, the vanquished prowess goes into the victor, then surely in that

mighty chest, those arms like necks of bulls, was the power of the thousand cattle he had downed in fight.

'Caramba! what a bear! Pedro was not so far astray.'

Sing—sing—sing! the lariats flew. *Swish—pat!* one, two, three, they fell. These were not men to miss. Three ropes, three horses, leaping away to bear on the great beast's neck. But swifter than thought the supple paws went up. The ropes were slipped, and the spurred cow-ponies, ready for the shock, went, shockless, bounding—loose ropes trailing afar.

'*Hi—Ha! Ho—Lan!* Head him!' as the Grizzly, liking not the unequal fight, made for the hills. But a deft Mexican in silver gear sent his hide riata whistling, then haunched his horse as the certain coil sank in the Grizzly's hock, and checked the Monarch with a heavy jar. Uttering one great snort of rage, he turned; his huge jaws crossed the rope, back nearly to his ears it went, and he ground it as a dog might grind a twig, so the straining pony bounded free.

Round and round him now the riders swooped, waiting their chance. More than once his neck was caught, but he slipped the noose as though it were all play. Again he was caught by a foot and wrenched, almost thrown, by the weight of two strong steeds, and now he foamed in rage. Memories of olden days, or more likely the habit of olden days, came on him—days when he learned to strike the yelping pack that dodged his blows. He was far from the burnt thicket, but a single bush was near, and setting his broad back to that, he waited for the circling foe. Nearer and nearer they urged the frightened steeds, and Monarch watched—waited, as of old, for the dogs, till they were almost touching each other, then he sprang like an avalanche of rock. What can elude a Grizzly's dash? The earth shivered as he launched himself, and trembled when he struck. Three men, three horses, in each other's way. The dust was thick; they only knew he struck—struck—struck! The horses never rose.

'Santa Maria!' came a cry of death, and hovering riders dashed to draw the bear away. Three horses dead, one man dead, one nearly so, and only one escaped.

Crack! crack! crack! went the pistols now as the bear went rocking his huge form in rapid charge for the friendly hills; and the four riders, urged by Kellyan, followed fast. They passed him, wheeled, face him. The pistols had wounded him in many places.

'Don't shoot—don't shoot, but tire him out,' the hunter urged.

'Tire him out? Look at Carlos and Manuel back there. How many minutes will it be before the rest are down with them?' So the infuriating pistols popped till all their shots were gone, and Monarch foamed with slobbering jaws of rage.

'Keep on! keep cool,' cried Kellyan.

His lariat flew as the cattle-killing paw was lifted for an instant. The lasso bound his wrist. *Sing! Sing!* went two, and caught him by the neck. A bull with his great club-foot in a noose is surely caught, but the Grizzly raised his supple, hand-like, tapering paw and gave one jerk that freed it. Now the two on his neck were tight; he could not slip them. The horses at the ends—they were dragging, choking him; men were shouting, hovering, watching for a new chance, when Monarch, firmly planting both paws, braced, bent those mighty shoulders, and, spite of shortening breath, leaned back on those two ropes as Samson did on pillars of the house of Baal, and straining horses with their riders were dragged forward more and more, long grooves being plowed behind; dragging them, he backed faster and faster still. His eyes were starting, his tongue lolling out.

'Keep on! hold tight!' was the cry, till the ropers swung together, the better to resist; and Monarch, big and strong with frenzied hate, seeing now his turn, sprang forward like a shot. The horses leaped and escaped—almost; the last was

one small inch too slow. The awful paw with jags of steel just grazed his flank. How slight it sounds! But what it really means is better not written down.

The riders had slipped their ropes in fear, and the Monarch, rumbling, snorting, bounding, trailed them to the hills, there to bite them off in peace, while the remnant of the gallant crew went, sadly muttering, back.

Bitter words went round. Kellyan was cursed.

'His fault. Why didn't we have the guns?'

'We were all in it,' was the answer, and more hard words, till Kellyan flushed, forgot his calm, and drew a pistol hitherto concealed, and the other 'took it back.'

15

The Cataract

'WHAT is next, Lan?' said Lou, as they sat dispirited by the fire that night.

Kellyan was silent for a time, then said slowly and earnestly, with a gleam in his eye: 'Lou, that's the greatest bear alive. When I seen him set up there like a butte and swat horses like they was flies, I jest loved him. He's the greatest thing God has turned loose in these yer hills. Before today, I sure wanted to get him; now, Lou, I'm a-going to get him, an' get him alive, if it takes all my natural days. I think I kin do it alone, but I know I kin do it with you,' and deep in Kellyan's eyes there glowed a little spark of something not yet rightly named.

They were camped in the hills, being no longer welcome at the ranch; the ranchers thought their price too high. Some even decided that the Monarch, being a terror to sheep, was not an undesirable neighbour. The cattle bounty was withdrawn, but the newspaper bounty was not.

'I want you to bring in that bear,' was the brief but pregnant message from the rich newsman when he heard of the fight with the riders.

'How are you going about it, Lan?'

Every bridge has its rotten plank, every fence its flimsy rail, every great one his weakness, and Kellyan, as he pondered, knew how mad it was to meet this one of brawn with mere brute force.

'Steel traps are no good; he smashes them. Lariats won't do, and he knows all about log traps. But I have a scheme. First, we must follow him up and learn his range. I reckon that'll take three months.'

So the two kept on. They took up that bear-trail next day; they found the lariats chewed off. They followed day after day. They learned what they could from rancher and sheep-herder, and much more was told them than they could believe.

Three months, Lan said, but it took six months to carry out his plan; meanwhile Monarch killed and killed.

In each section of his range they made one or two cage- or pen-traps of bolted logs. At the back end of each they put a small grating of heavy steel bars. The door was carefully made and fitted into grooves. It was of double plank, with tar-paper between to make it surely light-tight. It was sheeted with iron on the inside, and when it dropped it went into an iron-bound groove in the floor.

They left these traps open and unset till they were greyed with age and smelt no more of man. Then the two hunters prepared for the final play. They baited all without setting them—baited them with honey, the lure that Monarch never had refused—and when at length they found the honey baits were gone, they came where he now was taking toll and laid the long-planned snare. Every trap was set, and baited as before with a mass of honey—but *honey now mixed with a potent sleeping draught.*

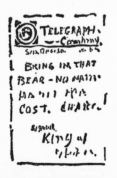

TELEGRAPH
Company

BRING IN THAT
BEAR - NO MATTER
WHAT THE
COST. CHASE.

King of
the west.

16

Landlocked

THAT night the great bear left his lair, one of his many lairs, and, cured of all his wounds, rejoicing in the fullness of his mighty strength, he strode towards the plains. His nose, ever alert, reported—sheep, a deer, a grouse; men—more sheep, some cows, and some calves; a bull—a fighting bull—and Monarch wheeled in big, rude, bearish joy at the coming battle brunt; but as he hugely hulked from hill to hill a different message came, so soft and low, so different from the smell of beefish brutes, one might well wonder he could sense it, but like a tiny ringing bell when thunder booms it came, and Monarch wheeled at once. Oh, it cast a potent spell! It stood for something very near to ecstasy with him, and down the hill and through the pines he went, on and on faster yet, abandoned to its sorcery. Here to its home he traced it, a long, low cavern. He had seen such many times before, had been held in them more than once, but had learned to spurn them. For weeks he had been robbing them of their treasures, and its odour, like a calling voice, was still his guide. Into the cavern he passed and it reeked with the smell of joy. There was the luscious mass, and Monarch, with all caution lulled

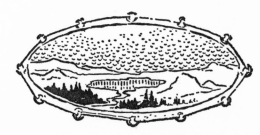

now, licked and licked, then seized to tear the bag for more, when down went the door with a low 'bang!' The Monarch started, but all was still and there was no smell of danger. He had forced such doors before. His palate craved the honey still, and he licked and licked, greedily at first, then calmly, then slowly, then drowsily—then at last stopped. His eyes were closing, and he sank slowly down on the earth and slept a heavy sleep.

Calm, but white-faced, were they—the men—when in the dawn they came. There were the huge scarred tracks inleading; there was the door down; there dimly they could see a mass of fur that filled the pen, that heaved in deepest sleep.

Strong ropes, strong chains and bands of steel were at hand, with chloroform, lest he should revive too soon. Through holes in the roof with infinite toil they chained him, bound him—his paws to his neck, his neck and breast and hind legs to a bolted beam. Then raising the door, they dragged him out, not with horses—none would go near—but with a windlass to a tree; and fearing the sleep of death, they let him now revive.

Chained and double chained, frenzied, foaming, and impotent, what words can tell the state of the fallen Monarch? They put him on a sled, and six horses with a long chain drew it by stages to the plain, to the railway. They fed him enough to save his life. A great steam-derrick lifted bear and beam and chain onto a flat-car, a tarpaulin was spread above his helpless form; the engine puffed, pulled out; and the Grizzly King was gone from his ancient hills.

So they brought him to the great city, the Monarch born, in chains. They put him in a cage not merely strong enough for a lion, but thrice as strong, and once a rope gave way as the huge one strained his bonds. 'He is loose,' went the cry, and an army of onlookers and keepers fled; only the small man with the calm eye and the big man of the hills were staunch, so the Monarch was still held.

Free in the cage, he swung round, looked this way and that, then heaved his powers against the triple angling steel and wrenched the cage so not a part of it was square. In time he clearly would break out. They dragged the prisoner to another that an elephant could not break down, but it stood on the ground, and in an hour the great beast had a cavern into the earth and was sinking out of sight, till a stream of water sent after him filled the hole and forced him again to view. They moved him to a new cage made for him since he came—a hard rock floor, great bars of nearly two-inch steel that reached up nine feet and then projected in for five. The Monarch wheeled once around, then, rearing, raised his ponderous bulk, wrenched those bars, unbreakable, and bent and turned them in their sockets with one heave till the five-foot spears were pointed out, and then sprang to climb. Nothing but pikes and blazing brands in a dozen ruthless hands could hold him back. The keepers watched him night and day till a stronger cage was made, impregnable with steel above and rocks below.

The Untamed One passed swiftly around, tried every bar, examined every corner, sought for a crack in the rocky floor, and found at last the place where was a six-inch timber beam—the only piece of wood in its frame. It was sheathed in iron, but exposed for an inch its whole length. One claw could reach the wood, and here he lay on his side and raked—raked all day till a great pile of shavings was lying by it and the beam sawn in two; but the cross-bolts remained, and when Monarch put his vast shoulder to the place it yielded not a whit. That was his last hope; now it was gone; and the huge bear sank down in the cage with his nose in his paws and sobbed—long, heavy sobs, animal sounds indeed, but telling just as truly as in man of the broken spirit—the hope and the life gone out. The keepers came with food at the appointed

time, but the bear moved not. They set it down, but in the morning it was still untouched. The bear was lying as before, his ponderous form in the pose he had first taken. The sobbing was replaced by a low moan at intervals.

Two days went by. The food, untouched, was corrupting in the sun. The third day, and Monarch still lay on his breast, his huge muzzle under his huger paw. His eyes were hidden; only a slight heaving of his broad chest was now seen.

'He is dying,' said one keeper. 'He can't live overnight.'

'Send for Kellyan,' said the another.

So Kellyan came, slight and thin. There was the beast that he had chained, pining, dying. He had sobbed his life out in his last hope's death, and a thrill of pity came over the hunter, for men of grit and power love grit and power. He put his arm through the cage bars and stroked him, but Monarch made no sign. His body was cold. At length a little moan was sign of life, and Kellyan said, 'Here, let me go in to him.'

'You are mad,' said the keepers, and they would not open the cage. But Kellyan persisted till they put in a cross-grating in front of the bear. Then, with this between, he approached. His hand was on the shaggy head, but Monarch lay as before. The hunter stroked his victim and spoke to him. His hand went to the big round ears, small above the head. They were rough to his touch. He looked again, then started. What! is it true? Yes, the stranger's tale was true, for both ears were pierced with a round hole—one torn large—and Kellyan knew that once again he had met his little Jack.

'Why, Jacky, I didn't know it was you. I never would have done it if I had known it was you. Jacky, old pard, don't you know me?'

But Jack stirred not, and Kellyan got up quickly. Back to the hotel he flew; there he put on his hunter's suit, smoky and smelling of pine gum and grease, and returned with a mass of honeycomb to re-enter the cage.

'Jacky, Jacky!' he cried, 'honey, honey!' and he held the tempting comb before him. But Monarch lay as one dead now.

'Jacky, Jacky! don't you know me?' He dropped the honey and laid his hands on the great muzzle.

The voice was forgotten. The old-time invitation, 'Honey, Jacky—honey,' had lost its power, but the *smell* of the honey, the coat, the hands that he had fondled, had together a hidden potency.

There is a time when the dying of our race forget their life, but clearly remember the scenes of childhood; these only are real and return with master power. And why not with a bear? The power of scent was there to call them back again, and Jacky, the Grizzly Monarch, raised his head a little—just a little; the eyes were nearly closed, but the big brown nose was jerked up feebly two or three times—the sign of interest that Jacky used to give in days of old. Now it was Kellyan that broke down even as the bear had done.

'I didn't know it was you, Jacky, or I never would have done it. Oh, Jacky, forgive me!' He rose and fled from the cage.

The keepers were there. They scarcely understood the scene, but one of them, acting on the hint, pushed the honey-comb nearer and cried, 'Honey, Jacky—honey!'

Filled by despair, he had lain down to die, but here was a new-born hope, not clear, not exact as words might put it, but his conqueror had shown himself a friend; this seemed a new hope, and the keeper, taking up the old call, 'Honey, Jacky—honey!' pushed the comb till it touched his muzzle. The smell was wafted to his sense, its message reached his brain; hope honoured, it must awake response. The great tongue licked the comb, appetite revived, and thus in new-born hope began the chapter of his gloom.

Skilful keepers were there with plans to meet the Monarch's every want. Delicate foods were offered and every shift was tried to tempt him back to strength and prison life.

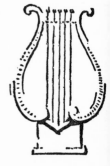

He ate and—lived.

And still he lives, but pacing—pacing—pacing—you may
see him, scanning not the crowds, but something beyond the
crowds, breaking down at times into petulant rages, but
recovering anon his ponderous dignity, looking—waiting—
watching—held ever by that hope, that unknown hope, that
came. Kellyan has been to him since, but Monarch knows him
not. Over his head, beyond him, was the great bear's gaze, far
away towards Tallac or far away on the sea, we knowing not
which or why, but pacing—pacing—pacing—held like the
storied Wandering One to a life of ceaseless journey—a
journey aimless, endless, and sad.

The wound-spots long ago have left his shaggy coat, but the
earmarks still are there, the ponderous strength, the elephan-
tine dignity. His eyes are dull—never were bright—but they
seem not vacant, and most often fixed on the Golden Gate
where the river seeks the sea.

The river, born in high Sierra's flank, that lived and rolled
and grew, through mountain pines, o'erleaping man-made
barriers, then to reach with growing power the plains and
bring its mighty flood at last to the Bay of Bays, a prisoner
there to lie, the prisoner of the Golden Gate, seeking forever
Freedom's Blue, seeking and raging—raging and seeking—
back and forth, forever—in vain.

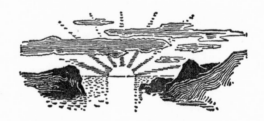

The Biography of a Grizzly

1

HE was born over a score of years ago, away up in the wildest part of the wild West, on the head of the Little Piney, above where the Palette Ranch is now.

His mother was just an ordinary Silvertip, living the quiet life that all bears prefer, minding her own business and doing her duty by her family, asking no favours of any one excepting to let her alone.

It was July before she took her remarkable family down the Little Piney to the Graybull, and showed them what strawberries were, and where to find them.

Notwithstanding their mother's deep conviction, the cubs were not remarkably big or bright; yet they were a remarkable family, for there were four of them, and it is not often a Grizzly mother can boast of more than two.

The woolly-coated little creatures were having a fine time, and revelled in the lovely mountain summer and the abundance of good things. Their mother turned over each log and flat stone they came to, and the moment it was lifted they all rushed under it like a lot of little pigs to lick up the ants and grubs there hidden.

It never once occurred to them that mother's strength might fail sometime, and let the great rock drop just as they got under it; nor would any one have thought so that might have chanced to see that huge arm and that shoulder sliding about under the great yellow robe she wore. No, no; that arm could never fail. The little ones were quite right. So they hustled and tumbled one another at each fresh log in their haste to be first, and squealed little squeals, and growled little growls, as if each was a pig, a pup, and a kitten all rolled into one.

They were well acquainted with the common little brown ants that harbour under logs in the uplands, but now they came for the first time on one of the hills of the great, fat, luscious Wood-ant, and they all crowded around to lick up those that ran out. But they soon found that they were licking up more cactus-prickles and sand than ants, till their mother said in Grizzly, 'Let me show you how.'

She knocked off the top of the hill, then laid her great paw flat on it for a few moments, and as the angry ants swarmed onto it she licked them up with one lick, and got a good rich mouthful to crunch, without a grain of sand or a cactus-stinger in it. The cubs soon learned. Each put up both his little brown paws, so that there was a ring of paws all around the ant-hill, and there they sat, like children playing 'hands,' and each licked first the right and then the left paw, or one cuffed his brother's ears for licking a paw that was not his own, till the ant-hill was cleared out and they were ready for a change.

Ants are sour food and made the bears thirsty, so the old one led down to the river. After they had drunk as much as they wanted, and dabbled their feet, they walked down the bank to a pool, where the old one's keen eye caught sight of a number of Buffalo-fish basking on the bottom. The water was very low, mere pebbly rapids between these deep holes, so Mammy said to the little ones:

'Now you all sit there on the bank and learn something new.'

First she went to the lower end of the pool and stirred up a cloud of mud which hung in the still water, and sent a long tail floating like a curtain over the rapids just below. Then she went quietly round by land, and sprang into the upper end of the pool with all the noise she could. The fish had crowded to that end, but this sudden attack sent them off in a panic, and they dashed blindly into the mud-cloud. Out of fifty fish there is always a good chance of some being fools, and half a dozen of these dashed through the darkened water into the current, and before they knew it they were struggling over the shingly shallow. The old Grizzly jerked them out to the bank, and the little ones rushed noisily on these funny, short snakes that could not get away, and gobbled and gorged till their little bellies looked like balloons.

They had eaten so much now, and the sun was so hot, that all were quite sleepy. So the mother bear led them to a quiet little nook, and as soon as she lay down, though they were puffing with heat, they all snuggled around her and went to sleep, with their little brown paws curled in, and their little black noses tucked into their wool as though it were a very cold day.

After an hour or two they began to yawn and stretch themselves, except little Fuzz, the smallest; she poked out her sharp nose for a moment, then snuggled back between her mother's great arms, for she was a gentle, petted little thing. The largest, the one afterwards known as Wahb, sprawled over on his back and began to worry a root that stuck up, grumbling to himself as he chewed it, or slapped it with his paw for not staying where he wanted it. Presently Mooney, the mischief, began tugging at Frizzle's ears, and got his own well boxed. They clenched for a tussle; then, locked in a tight, little grizzly yellow ball, they sprawled over and over on the grass, and, before they knew it, down a bank, and away out of sight towards the river.

Almost immediately there was an outcry of yells for help from the little wrestlers. There could be no mistaking the real terror in their voices. Some dreadful danger was threatening.

Up jumped the gentle mother, changed into a perfect demon, and over the bank in time to see a huge Range-bull make a deadly charge at what he doubtless took for a yellow dog. In a moment all would have been over with Frizzle, for he had missed his footing on the bank; but there was a thumping of heavy feet, a roar that startled even the great bull, and, like a huge bounding ball of yellow fur, Mother Grizzly was upon him. Him! the monarch of the herd, the master of all these plains, what had he to fear? He bellowed his deep war-cry, and charged to pin the old one to the bank; but as he bent to tear her with his shining horns, she dealt him a stunning blow, and before he could recover she was on his shoulders, raking the flesh from his ribs with sweep after sweep of her terrific claws.

The bull roared with rage, and plunged and reared, dragging Mother Grizzly with him; then, as he hurled heavily off the slope, she let go to save herself, and the bull rolled down into the river.

This was a lucky thing for him, for the Grizzly did not want to follow him there; so he waded out on the other side, and bellowing with fury and pain, slunk off to join the herd to which he belonged.

2

OLD Colonel Pickett, the cattle king, was out riding the range. The night before, he had seen the new moon descending over the white cone of Pickett's Peak.

'I saw the last moon over Frank's Peak,' said he, 'and the luck was against me for a month; now I reckon it's my turn.'

Next morning his luck began. A letter came from Washington granting his request that a post office be established at his ranch, and contained the polite inquiry, 'What name do you suggest for the new post office?'

The Colonel took down his new rifle, a 45–90 repeater. 'May as well,' he said; 'this is my month.' And he rode up the Greybull to see how the cattle were doing.

As he passed under the Rimrock Mountain he heard a far-away roarings as of bulls fighting, but thought nothing of it till he rounded the point and saw on the flat below a lot of his cattle pawing the dust and bellowing as they always do when they smell the blood of one of the number. He soon saw that the great bull, 'the boss of the bunch,' was covered with blood. His back and sides were torn as by a Mountain lion, and his head was battered as by another bull.

'Grizzly,' growled the Colonel, for he knew the mountains. He quickly noted the general direction of the bull's back trail, then rode towards a high bank that offered a view. This was across the gravelly ford of the Greybull, near the mouth of the Piney. His horse splashed through the cold water and began jerkily to climb the other bank.

As soon as the rider's head rose above the bank his hand grabbed the rifle, for there in full sight were five Grizzly bears, an old one and four cubs.

'Run for the woods,' growled the Mother Grizzly, for she knew that men carried guns. Not that she feared for herself; but the idea of such things among her darlings was too horrible to think of. She set off to guide them to the timber-tangle on the Lower Piney. But an awful, murderous fusillade began.

Bang! and Mother Grizzly felt a deadly pang.

Bang! and poor little Fuzz rolled over with a scream of pain and lay still.

With a roar of hate and fury Mother Grizzly turned to attack the enemy.

Bang! and she fell paralyzed and dying with a high shoulder shot. And the three little cubs, not knowing what to do, ran back to their mother.

Bang! bang! and Mooney and Frizzle sank in dying agonies beside her, and Wahb, terrified and stupefied ran in a circle about them. Then, hardly knowing why, he turned and dashed into the timber-tangle, and disappeared as a last *bang* left him with a stinging pain and a useless, broken hind paw.

THAT is why the post office was called Four-Bears. The Colonel seemed pleased with what he had done; indeed, he told of it himself.

But away up in the woods of Anderson's Peak that night a little lame Grizzly might have been seen wandering, limping along, leaving a bloody spot each time he tried to set down his hind paw; whining and whimpering, 'Mother! Mother! Oh, Mother, where are you?' for he was cold and hungry, and had such a pain in his foot. But there was no mother to come to him, and he dared not go back where he had left her, so he wandered aimlessly about among the pines.

Then he smelled some strange animal smell and heard heavy footsteps; and not knowing what else to do, he climbed a tree. Presently a band of great, long-necked, slim-legged animals, taller than his mother, came by under the tree. He had seen such once before and had not been afraid of them then, because he had been with his mother. But now he kept very quiet in the tree, and the big creatures stopped picking the grass when they were near him, and blowing their noses, ran out of sight.

He stayed in the tree till near morning, and then he was so stiff with cold that he could scarcely get down. But the warm sun came up, and he felt better as he sought about for berries and ants, for he was very hungry. Then he went back to the Piney and put his wounded foot in the ice-cold water.

He wanted to get back to the mountains again, but still he felt he must go to where he had left his mother and brothers. When the afternoon grew warm, he went limping down the stream through the timber, and down on the banks of the Greybull till he came to the place where yesterday they had had the fish-feast; and he eagerly crunched the heads and remains that he found. But there was an odd and horrid smell on the wind. It frightened him, and as he went down to where he last had seen his mother the smell grew worse. He peeped out cautiously at the place, and saw there a lot of Coyotes, tearing at something. What it was he did not know; but he saw no mother, and the smell that sickened and terrified

him was worse than ever, so he quietly turned back towards the timber-tangle of the Lower Piney, and nevermore came back to look for his lost family. He wanted his mother as much as ever, but something told him it was no use.

As cold night came down, he missed her more and more again, and he whimpered as he limped along, a miserable, lonely, little, motherless bear—not lost in the mountains, for he had no home to seek, but so sick and lonely, and with such a pain in his foot and in his stomach a craving for the drink that would nevermore be his. That night he found a hollow log, and crawling in, he tried to dream that his mother's great, furry arms were around him, and he snuffled himself to sleep.

3

WAHB had always been a gloomy little bear; and the string of misfortunes that came on him just as his mind was forming made him more than ever sullen and morose.

It seemed as though every one were against him. He tried to keep out of sight in the upper woods of the Piney, seeking his food by day and resting at night in the hollow log. But one evening he found it occupied by a porcupine as big as himself and as bad as a cactus-bush. Wahb could do nothing with him. He had to give up the log and seek another nest.

One day he went down on the Greybull flat to dig some roots that his mother had taught him were good. But before he had well begun, a greyish-looking animal came out of a hole in the ground and rushed at him, hissing and growling. Wahb did not know it was a badger, but he saw it was a fierce animal as big as himself. He was sick, and lame too, so he limped away and never stopped till he was on a ridge in the next canyon. Here a coyote saw him, and came bounding after him, calling at the same time to another to come and join the fun. Wahb was near a tree, so he scrambled up to the branches. The coyotes came bounding and yelping below, but

their noses told them that this was a young Grizzly they had chased, and they soon decided that a young Grizzly in a tree means a Mother Grizzly not far away, and they had better let him alone.

After they had sneaked off Wahb came down and returned to the Piney. There was better feeding on the Greybull, but every one seemed against him there now that his loving guardian was gone, while on the Piney he had peace at least sometimes, and there were plenty of trees that he could climb when an enemy came.

His broken foot was a long time in healing; indeed, it never got quite well. The wound healed and the soreness wore off, but it left a stiffness that gave him a slight limp, and the sole-balls grew together quite unlike those of the other foot. It particularly annoyed him when he had to climb a tree or run fast from his enemies; and of them he found no end, though never once did a friend cross his path. When he lost his mother he lost his best and only friend. She would have taught him much that he had to learn by bitter experience, and would have saved him from most of the ills that befell him in his cubhood—ills so many and so dire that but for his native sturdiness he never could have passed through alive.

The piñons bore plentifully that year, and the winds began to shower down the ripe, rich nuts. Life was becoming a little easier for Wahb. He was gaining in health and strength, and the creatures he daily met now let him alone. But as he feasted on the piñons one morning after a gale, a great Black-bear came marching down the hill. 'No one meets a friend in the woods,' was a byword that Wahb had learned already. He swung up the nearest tree. At first the Blackbear was scared, for he smelled the smell of Grizzly; but when he saw it was only a cub, he took courage and came growling at Wahb. He could climb as well as the little Grizzly, or better, and high as Wahb went, the Blackbear followed, and when

Wahb got out on the smallest and highest twig that would carry him, the Blackbear cruelly shook him off, so that he was thrown to the ground, bruised and shaken and half-stunned. He limped away moaning, and the only thing that kept the Blackbear from following him up and perhaps killing him was the fear that the old Grizzly might be about. So Wahb was driven away down the creek from all the good piñon woods.

There was not much food on the Greybull now. The berries were nearly all gone; there were no fish or ants to get, and Wahb, hurt, lonely, and miserable, wandered on and on, till he was away down towards the Meteetsee.

A coyote came bounding and barking through the sage-brush after him. Wahb tried to run, but it was no use; the coyote was soon up with him. Then with a sudden rush of desperate courage Wahb turned and charged his foe. The astonished coyote gave a scared yowl or two, and fled with his tail between his legs. Thus Wahb learned that war is the price of peace.

But the forage was poor here; there were too many cattle; and Wahb was making for a far-away piñon woods in the Meteetsee Canyon when he saw a man, just like the one he had seen on that day of sorrow. At the same moment he heard a *bang*, and some sage-brush rattled and fell just over his back. All the dreadful smells and dangers of that day came back to his memory, and Wahb ran as he never had run before.

He soon got into a gully and followed it into the canyon. An opening between two cliffs seemed to offer shelter, but as he ran towards it a Range-cow came trotting between, shaking her head at him and snorting threats against his life.

He leaped aside upon a long log that led up a bank, but at once a savage bobcat appeared on the other end and warned him to go back. It was no time to quarrel. Bitterly Wahb felt that the world was full of enemies. But he turned and scrambled

up a rocky bank into the piñon woods that border the benches of the Meteetsee.

The Pine squirrels seemed to resent his coming, and barked furiously. They were thinking about their piñon-nuts. They knew that this bear was coming to steal their provisions, and they followed him overhead to scold and abuse him, with such an outcry that an enemy might have followed him by their noise, which was exactly what they intended.

There was no one following, but it made Wahb uneasy and nervous. So he kept on till he reached the timber line, where both food and foes were scarce, and here on the edge of the Mountain-sheep land at last he got a chance to rest.

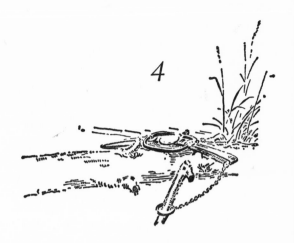

4

WAHB never was sweet-tempered like his baby sister, and the persecutions by his numerous foes were making him more and more sour. Why could not they let him alone in his misery? Why was every one against him? If only he had his mother back! If he could only have killed that Blackbear that had driven him from his woods! It did not occur to him that some day he himself would be big. And that spiteful bobcat, that took advantage of him; and the man that had tried to kill him. He did not forget any of them, and he hated them all.

Wahb found his new range fairly good, because it was a good nut year. He learned just what the squirrels feared he would, for his nose directed him to the little granaries where they had stored up great quantities of nuts for winter's use. It was hard on the squirrels, but it was good luck for Wahb, for the nuts were delicious food. And when the days shortened and the nights began to be frosty, he had grown fat and well-favoured.

He travelled over all parts of the canyon now, living mostly in the higher woods, but coming down at times to forage almost as far as the river. One night as he wandered by the

deep water a peculiar smell reached his nose. It was quite
pleasant, so he followed it up to the water's edge. It seemed
to come from a sunken log. As he reached over towards this,
there was a sudden *clank*, and one of his paws was caught in a
strong, steel beaver trap.

Wahb yelled and jerked back with all his strength, and tore
up the stake that held the trap. He tried to shake it off, then
ran away through the bushes trailing it. He tore at it with his
teeth; but there it hung, quiet, cold, strong, and immovable.
Every little while he tore at it with his teeth and claws, or
beat it against the ground. He buried it in the earth, then
climbed a low tree, hoping to leave it behind; but still it
clung, biting into his flesh. He made for his own woods, and
sat down to try to puzzle it out. He did not know what it was,
but his little green-brown eyes glared with a mixture of pain,
fright, and fury as he tried to understand his new enemy.

He lay down under the bushes, and, intent on deliberately
crushing the thing, he held it down with one paw while he
tightened his teeth on the other end, and bearing down as it
slid away, the trap jaws opened and the foot was free. It was
mere chance, of course, that led him to squeeze both springs
at once. He did not understand it, but he did not forget it,
and he got these not very clear ideas: 'There is a dreadful little
enemy that hides by the water and waits for one. It has an odd
smell. It bites one's paws and is too hard for one to bite. But
it can be got off by hard squeezing.'

For a week or more the little Grizzly had another sore paw,
but it was not very bad if he did not do any climbing.

It was now the season when the elk were bugling on the
mountains. Wahb heard them all night, and once or twice had
to climb to get away from one of the big-antlered bulls. It was
also the season when the trappers were coming into the
mountains, and the wild geese were honking overhead. There
were several quite new smells in the woods, too. Wahb

followed one of these up, and it led to a place where were some small logs piled together; then, mixed with the smell that had drawn him, was one that he hated—he remembered it from the time when he had lost his mother. He sniffed about carefully, for it was not very strong, and learned that this hateful smell was on a log in front, and the sweet smell that made his mouth water was under some brush behind. So he went around, pulled away the brush till he got the prize, a piece of meat, and as he grabbed it, the log in front went down with a heavy *chock*.

It made Wahb jump; but he got away all right with the meat and some new ideas, and with one old idea made stronger, and that was, 'When that hateful smell is around it always means trouble.'

As the weather grew colder, Wahb became very sleepy; he slept all day when it was frosty. He had not any fixed place to sleep in; he knew a number of dry ledges for sunny weather, and one or two sheltered nooks for stormy days. He had a very comfortable nest under a root, and one day, as it began to blow and snow, he crawled into this and curled up to sleep. The storm howled without. The snow fell deeper and deeper. It draped the pine-trees till they bowed, then shook themselves clear to be draped anew. It drifted over the mountains and poured down the funnel-like ravines, blowing off the peaks and ridges, and filling up the hollows level with their rims. It piled up over Wahb's den, shutting out the cold of the winter, shutting out itself: and Wahb slept and slept.

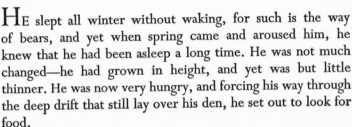

5

HE slept all winter without waking, for such is the way of bears, and yet when spring came and aroused him, he knew that he had been asleep a long time. He was not much changed—he had grown in height, and yet was but little thinner. He was now very hungry, and forcing his way through the deep drift that still lay over his den, he set out to look for food.

There were no piñon nuts to get, and no berries or ants; but Wahb's nose led him away up the canyon to the body of a winter-killed elk, where he had a fine feast, and then buried the rest for future use.

Day after day he came back till he had finished it. Food was very scarce for a couple of months, and after the elk was eaten, Wahb lost all the fat he had when he awoke. One day he climbed over the Divide into the Warhouse Valley. It was warm and sunny there, vegetation was well advanced, and he found good forage. He wandered down towards the thick timber, and soon smelled the smell of another Grizzly. This grew stronger and led him to a single tree by a bear-trail. Wahb reared up on his hind feet to smell this tree. It was strong of bear, and was plastered with mud and Grizzly hair far higher than he could reach; and Wahb knew that it must have been a very large bear that had rubbed himself there. He felt uneasy. He used to long to meet one of his own kind, yet now that there was a chance of it he was filled with dread.

No one had shown him anything but hatred in his lonely, unprotected life, and he could not tell what this older bear might do. As he stood in doubt, he caught sight of the old Grizzly himself slouching along a hillside, stopping from time to time to dig up the quamash-roots and wild turnips.

He was a monster. Wahb instinctively distrusted him, and sneaked away through the woods and up a rocky bluff where he could watch.

Then the big fellow came on Wahb's track and rumbled a deep growl of anger; he followed the trail to the tree, and rearing up, he tore the bark with his claws, far above where Wahb had reached. Then he strode rapidly along Wahb's trail. But the cub had seen enough. He fled back over the Divide into the Meteetsee Canyon, and realized in his dim, bearish way that he was at peace there because the bear-forage was so poor.

As the summer came on, his coat was shed. His skin got very itchy, and he found pleasure in rolling in the mud and scraping his back against some convenient tree. He never climbed now: his claws were too long, and his arms, though growing big and strong, were losing that suppleness of wrist that makes cub Grizzlies and all Blackbears great climbers. He now dropped naturally into the bear habit of seeing how high he could reach with his nose on the rubbing-post, whenever he was near one.

He may not have noticed it, yet each time he came to a post, after a week or two away, he could reach higher, for Wahb was growing fast and coming into his strength.

Sometimes he was at one end of the country that he felt

was his, and sometimes at another, but he had frequent use for the rubbing-tree, and thus it was that his range was mapped out by posts with his own mark on them.

One day late in summer he sighted a stranger on his land, a glossy Blackbear, and he felt furious against the interloper. As the Blackbear came nearer Wahb noticed the tan-red face, the white spot on his breast, and then the bit out of his ear, and last of all the wind brought a whiff. There could be no further doubt it was the very smell: this was the black coward that had chased him down the Piney long ago. But how he had shrunken! Before, he had looked like a giant; now Wahb felt he could crush him with one paw. Revenge is sweet, Wahb felt, though he did not exactly say it, and he went for that red-nosed bear. But the Black one went up a small tree like a squirrel. Wahb tried to follow as the other once followed him, but somehow he could not. He did not seem to know how to take hold now, and after a while he gave it up and went away, although the Blackbear brought him back more than once by coughing in derision. Later on that day, when the Grizzly passed again, the red-nosed one had gone.

As the summer waned, the upper forage-grounds began to give out, and Wahb ventured down to the Lower Meteetsee one night to explore. There was a pleasant odour on the breeze, and following it up, Wahb came to the carcass of a steer. A good distance away from it were some tiny coyotes, mere dwarfs compared with those he remembered. Right by the carcass was another that jumped about in the moonlight in a foolish way. For some strange reason it seemed unable to get away. Wahb's old hatred broke out. He rushed up. In a flash the coyote bit him several times before, with one blow of that great paw, Wahb smashed him into a limp, furry rag; then broke in all his ribs with a crunch or two of his jaws. Oh, but it was good to feel the hot, bloody juices oozing between his teeth!

The coyote was caught in a trap. Wahb hated the smell of the iron, so he went to the other side of the carcass, where it was not so strong, and had eaten but little before *clank*, and his foot was caught in a wolf-trap that he had not seen.

But he remembered that he had once before been caught and had escaped by squeezing the trap. He set a hind foot on each spring and pressed till the trap opened and released his paw. About the carcass was the smell that he knew stood for man, so he left it and wandered down-stream; but more and more often he got whiffs of that horrible odour, so he turned and went back to his quiet piñon benches.

6

WAHB'S third summer had brought him the stature of a
large-sized bear, though not nearly the bulk and power
that in time were his. He was very light-coloured now, and
this was why Spahwat, a Shoshone Indian who more than once
hunted him, called him the Whitebear, or Wahb.

Spahwat was a good hunter, and as soon as he saw the rubbing
tree on the Upper Meteetsee he knew that he was on the
range of a big Grizzly. He bushwhacked the whole valley, and
spent many days before he found a chance to shoot; then
Wahb got a stinging flesh wound in the shoulder. He growled
horribly, but it had seemed to take the fight out of him; he
scrambled up the valley and over the lower hills till he reached
a quiet haunt, where he lay down.

His knowledge of healing was wholly instinctive. He licked
the wound and all around it, and sought to be quiet. The licking
removed the dirt, and by massage reduced the inflammation,
and it plastered the hair down as a sort of dressing over the
wound to keep out the air, dirt, and microbes. There could be
no better treatment.

But the Indian was on his trail. Before long the smell warned

. . . a savage bobcat appeared . . . (see page 81)

Wahb that a foe was coming, so he quietly climbed farther up the mountain to another resting-place. But again he sensed the Indian's approach, and made off. Several times this happened, and at length there was a second shot and another galling wound. Wahb was furious now. There was nothing that really frightened him but that horrible odour of man, iron, and guns, that he remembered from the day when he lost his mother; but now all fear of these left him. He heaved painfully up the mountain again, and along under a six-foot ledge, then up and back to the top of the bank, where he lay flat. On came the Indian, armed with knife and gun; deftly, swiftly keeping on the trail; gloating joyfully over each bloody print that meant such anguish to the hunted bear. Straight up the slide of broken rock he came, where Wahb, ferocious with pain, was waiting on the ledge. On sneaked the dogged hunter; his eye still scanned the bloody slots or swept the woods ahead, but never was raised to glance above the ledge. And Wahb, as he saw this shape of death relentless on his track, and smelled the hated smell, poised his bulk at heavy cost upon his quivering, mangled arm, there held until the proper instant came, then to his sound arm's matchless native force he added all the weight of desperate hate as down he struck one fearful, crushing blow. The Indian sank without a cry, and then dropped out of sight. Wahb rose, and sought again a quiet nook where he might nurse his wounds. Thus he learned that one must fight for peace; for he never saw that Indian again, and he had time to rest and recover.

7

THE years went on as before, except that each winter Wahb slept less soundly, and each spring he came out earlier and was a bigger Grizzly, with fewer enemies that dared to face him. When his sixth year came he was a very big, strong, sullen bear, with neither friendship nor love in his life since that evil day on the Lower Piney.

No one ever heard of Wahb's mate. No one believes that he ever had one. The love-season of bears came and went year after year, but left him alone in his prime as he had been in his youth. It is not good for a bear to be alone; it is bad for him in every way. His habitual moroseness grew with his strength, and any one chancing to meet him now would have called him a dangerous Grizzly.

He had lived in the Meteetsee Valley since first he betook himself there, and his character had been shaped by many little adventures with traps and his wild rivals of the mountains. But there was none of the latter that he now feared and he knew enough to avoid the first, for that penetrating odour of man and iron was a never-failing warning, especially after an experience which befell him in his sixth year.

His ever-reliable nose told him that there was a dead elk down among the timber.

He went up the wind, and there, sure enough, was the great delicious carcass, already torn open at the very best place. True, there was that terrible man-and-iron taint, but it was so slight and the feast so tempting that after circling around and inspecting the carcass from his eight feet of stature, as he stood erect, he went cautiously forward, and at once was caught by his left paw in an enormous bear-trap. He roared with pain and slashed about in a fury. But this was no beaver-trap; it was a big forty-pound bear-catcher, and he was surely caught.

Wahb fairly foamed with rage, and madly grit his teeth upon the trap. Then he remembered his former experiences. He placed the trap between his hind legs, with a hind paw on each spring, and pressed down with all his weight. But it was not enough. He dragged off the trap and its clog, and went clanking up the mountain. Again and again he tried to free his foot, but in vain, till he came where a great trunk crossed the trail a few feet from the ground. By chance, or happy thought, he reared again under this and made a new attempt. With a hind foot on each spring and his mighty shoulders underneath the tree, he bore down with his titanic strength: the great steel springs gave way, the jaws relaxed, and he tore out his foot. So Wahb was free again, though he left behind a great toe which had been nearly severed by the first snap of the steel.

Again Wahb had a painful wound to nurse, and as he was a left-handed bear—that is, when he wished to turn a rock over he stood on the right paw and turned with the left—one result of this disablement was to rob him for a time of all those dainty foods that are found under rocks or logs. The wound healed at last, but he never forgot that experience, and thenceforth the pungent smell of man and iron, even without the gun smell, never failed to enrage him.

Many experiences had taught him that it is better to run if he only smelled the hunter or heard him far away, but to fight desperately if the man was close at hand. And the cowboys soon came to know that the Upper Meteetsee was the range of a bear that was better let alone.

8

ONE day after a long absence Wahb came into the lower part of his range, and saw to his surprise one of the wooden dens that men make for themselves. As he came around to get the wind, he sensed the taint that never failed to infuriate him now, and a moment later he heard a loud *bang* and felt a stinging shock in his left hind leg, the old stiff leg. He wheeled about, in time to see a man running towards the new-made shanty. Had the shot been in his shoulder Wahb would have been helpless, but it was not.

MIGHTY arms that could toss pine logs like broomsticks, paws that with one tap could crush the biggest bull upon the range, claws that could tear huge slabs of rock from the mountainside —what was even the deadly rifle to them!

WHEN the man's partner came home that night he found him on the reddened shanty floor. The bloody trail from outside and a shaky, scribbled note on the back of a paper novel told the tale.

It was Wahb done it. I seen him by the spring and wounded him. I tried to git on the shanty, but he ketched me. My God, how I suffer!   JACK.

It was all fair. The man had invaded the bear's country, had tried to take the bear's life, and had lost his own. But Jack's partner swore he would kill that bear.

He took up the trail and followed it up the canyon, and there bush-whacked and hunted day after day. He put out baits and traps, and at length one day he heard a *crash*, *clatter*, *thump*, and a huge rock bounded down a bank into a wood, scaring out a couple of deer that floated away like thistledown. Miller thought at first that it was a land-slide; but he soon knew that it was Wahb that had rolled the boulder over merely for the sake of two or three ants beneath it.

The wind had not betrayed him, so on peering through the bush Miller saw the great bear as he fed, favouring his left hind leg and growling sullenly to himself at a fresh twinge of pain. Miller steadied himself, and thought, 'Here goes a finisher or a dead miss.' He gave a sharp whistle, the bear stopped every move, and, as he stood with ears acock, the man fired at his head.

But at that moment the great shaggy head moved, only an infuriating scratch was given, the smoke betrayed the man's place, and the Grizzly made savage, three-legged haste to catch his foe.

Miller dropped his gun and swung lightly into a tree, the only large one near. Wahb raged in vain against the trunk. He tore off the bark with his teeth and claws; but Miller was safe beyond his reach. For fully four hours the Grizzly watched, then gave it up, and slowly went off into the bushes till lost to view. Miller watched him from the tree, and afterwards waited nearly an hour to be sure that the bear was gone. He then slipped to the ground, got his gun, and set out for camp. But Wahb was cunning; he had only *seemed* to go away, and then had sneaked back quietly to watch. As soon as the man was away from the tree, too far to return, Wahb dashed after him. In spite of his wounds the bear could move the faster.

Within a quarter of a mile—well, Wahb did just what the man had sworn to do to him.

Long afterwards his friends found the gun and enough to tell the tale.

The claim-shanty on the Meteetsee fell to pieces. It never again was used, for no man cared to enter a country that had but few allurements to offset its evident curse of ill luck, and where such a terrible Grizzly was always on the war-path.

9

THEN they found good gold on the Upper Meteetsee. Miners came in pairs and wandered through the peaks, rooting up the ground and spoiling the little streams—grizzly old men mostly, that had lived their lives in the mountain and were themselves slowly turning into Grizzly bears; digging and grubbing everywhere, not for good, wholesome roots, but for that shiny yellow sand that they could not eat; living the lives of Grizzlies, asking nothing but to be let alone to dig.

They seemed to understand Grizzly Wahb. The first time they met, Wahb reared up on his hind legs, and the wicked green lightnings began to twinkle in his small eyes. The elder man said to his mate:

'Let him alone, and he won't bother you.'

'Ain't he an awful size, though?' replied the other, nervously.

Wahb was about to charge, but something held him back— a something that had no reference to his senses, that was felt only when they were still; a something that in bear and man is wiser than his wisdom, and that points the way at every doubtful fork in the dim and winding trail.

Of course Wahb did not understand what the men said, but

he did feel that there was something different here. The smell of man and iron was there, but not of that maddening kind, and he missed the pungent odour that even yet brought back the dark days of his cubhood.

The men did not move, so Wahb rumbled a subterranean growl, dropped down on his four feet, and went on.

Late the same year Wahb ran across the red-nosed Blackbear. How that bear did keep on shrinking! Wahb could have hurled him across the Greybull with one tap now.

But the Blackbear did not mean to let him try. He hustled his fat, podgy body up a tree at a rate that made him puff. Wahb reached up nine feet from the ground, and with one rake of his huge claws tore off the bark clear to the shining white wood and down nearly to the ground; and the Blackbear shivered and whimpered with terror as the scraping of those awful claws ran up the trunk and up his spine in a way that was horribly suggestive.

What was it that the sight of that Blackbear stirred in Wahb? Was it memories of the Upper Piney, long forgotten; thoughts of a woodland rich in food?

Wahb left him trembling up there as high as he could get, and without any very clear purpose swung along the upper benches of the Meteetsee down to the Greybull, around the foot of the Rimrock Mountain; on, till hours later he found himself in the timber-tangle of the Lower Piney, and among the berries and ants of the old times.

He had forgotten what a fine land the Piney was: plenty of food, no miners to spoil the streams, no hunters to keep an eye on, and no mosquitoes or flies, but plenty of open, sunny glades and sheltering woods, backed up by high, straight cliffs to turn the colder winds.

There were, moreover, no resident Grizzlies, no signs even of passing travellers, and the Blackbears that were in possession did not count.

Wahb was well pleased. He rolled his vast bulk in an old buffalo-wallow, and rearing up against a tree where the Piney Canyon quits the Greybull Canon, he left on it his mark fully eight feet from the ground.

In the days that followed he wandered farther and farther up among the rugged spurs of the Shoshones, and took possession as he went. He found the signboards of several Blackbears, and if they were small dead trees he sent them crashing to earth with a drive of his giant paw. If they were green, he put his own mark over the other mark, and made it clearer by slashing the bark with the great pickaxes that grew on his toes.

The Upper Piney had so long been a Blackbear range that the squirrels had ceased storing their harvest in hollow trees, and were now using the spaces under flat rocks, where the Black-bears could not get at them; so Wahb found this a land of plenty: every fourth or fifth rock in the pine woods was the roof of a squirrel or chipmunk granary, and when he turned it over, if the little owner were there, Wahb did not scruple to flatten him with his paw and devour him as an agreeable relish to his own provisions.

And wherever Wahb went he put up his sign-board:

Trespassers beware!

It was written on the trees as high up as he could reach, and every one that came by understood that the scent of it and the hair in it were those of the great Grizzly Wahb.

If his mother had lived to train him, Wahb would have known that a good range in spring may be a bad one in summer. Wahb found out by years of experience that a total change with the seasons is best. In the early spring the cattle and elk ranges, with their winter-killed carcasses, offer a bountiful feast. In early summer the best forage is on the warm hillsides where the quamash and the Indian turnip grow. In late summer the berry-bushes along the river-flat are laden with fruit, and

in autumn the pine woods gave good chances to fatten for the
winter. So he added to his range each year. He not only cleared
out the Blackbears from the Piney and the Meteetsee, but he
went over the Divide and killed that old fellow that had once
chased him out of the Warhouse Valley. And, more than that,
he held what he had won, for he broke up a camp of tenderfeet
that were looking for a ranch location on the Middle Meteetsee; he stampeded their horses, and made general smash of
the camp. And so all the animals, including man, came to know
that the whole range from Frank's Peak to the Shoshone spurs
was the proper domain of a king well able to defend it, and
the name of that king was Meteetsee Wahb.

Any creature whose strength puts him beyond danger of
open attack is apt to lose in cunning. Yet Wahb never forgot
his early experience with the traps. He made it a rule never
to go near that smell of man and iron, and that was the reason
that he never again was caught.

So he led his lonely life and slouched around on the mountains, throwing boulders about like pebbles, and huge trunks
like matchwood, as he sought for his daily food. And every
beast of hill and plain soon came to know and fly in fear of
Wahb, the one time hunted, persecuted cub. And more than
one Blackbear paid with his life for the ill-deed of that other,
long ago. And many a cranky bobcat flying before him took to
a tree, and if that tree were dead and dry, Wahb heaved it
down, and tree and cat alike were dashed to bits. Even the
proud-necked stallion, leader of the mustang band, thought
well for once to yield the road. The great grey Timberwolves,
and the Mountain lions too, left their new kill and sneaked in
sullen fear aside when Wahb appeared. And if, as he hulked
across the sage-covered river-flat sending the scared antelope
skimming like birds before him, he was faced perchance, by
some burly Range-bull, too young to be wise and too big to
be afraid, Wahb smashed his skull with one blow of that giant

paw, and served him as the Range-cow would have served himself long years ago.

The all-mother never fails to offer to her own, twin cups, one gall, and one of balm. Little or much they may drink, but equally of each. The mountain that is easy to descend must soon be climbed again. The grinding hardship of Wahb's early days, had built his mighty frame. All usual pleasures of a Grizzly's life had been denied him but *power* bestowed in more than double share.

So he lived on year after year, unsoftened by mate or companion, sullen, fearing nothing, ready to fight, but asking only to be let alone—quite alone. He had but one keen pleasure in his sombre life—the lasting glory in his matchless strength— the small but never failing thrill of joy as the foe fell crushed and limp, or the riven boulders grit and heaved when he turned on them the measure of his wondrous force.

10

EVERYTHING has a smell of its own for those that have
noses to smell. Wahb had been learning smells all his life,
and knew the meaning of most of those in the mountains. It
was as though each and every thing had a voice of its own for
him; and yet it was far better than a voice, for every one
knows that a good nose is better than eyes and ears together.
And each of these myriads of voices kept on crying, 'Here and
such am I.'

The juniper-berries, the rosehips, the strawberries, each had a
soft, sweet little voice, calling, 'Here we are—Berries, Berries.'

The great pine woods had a loud, far-reaching voice, 'Here
are we, the Pine trees,' but when he got right up to them
Wahb could hear the low, sweet call of the piñon-nuts, 'Here
are we, the Piñon-nuts.'

And the quamash beds in May sang a perfect chorus when the
wind was right: 'Quamash beds, Quamash beds.'

And when he got among them he made out each single voice.
Each root had its own little piece to say to his nose: 'Here
am I, a big Quamash, rich and ripe,' or a tiny, sharp voice,
'Here am I, a good-for-nothing, stringy little root.'

And the broad, rich russulas in the autumn called aloud, 'I am a fat, wholesome Mushroom,' and the deadly amanita cried, 'I am an Amanita. Let me alone, or you'll be a sick bear.' And the fairy harebell of the canyon-banks sang a song too, as fine as its thread-like stem, and as soft as its dainty blue; but the warden of the smells had learned to report it not, for this, and a million other such, were of no interest to Wahb.

So every living thing that moved, and every flower that grew, and every rock and stone and shape on earth told out its tale and sang its little story to his nose. Day or night, fog or bright, that great, moist nose told him most of the things he needed to know, or passed unnoticed those of no concern, and he depended on it more and more. If his eyes and ears together reported so and so, he would not even then believe it until his nose said, 'Yes; that is right.'

But this is something that man cannot understand, for he has sold the birthright of his nose for the privilege of living in towns.

While hundreds of smells were agreeable to Wahb, thousands were indifferent to him, a good many were unpleasant, and some actually put him in a rage.

He had often noticed that if a west wind were blowing when he was at the head of the Piney Canyon there was an odd, new scent. Some days he did not mind it, and some days it disgusted him; but he never followed it up. On other days a north wind from the high Divide brought a most awful smell, something unlike any other, a smell that he wanted only to get away from.

Wahb was getting well past his youth now, and he began to have pains in the hind leg that had been wounded so often. After a cold night or a long time of wet weather he could scarcely use that leg, and one day, while thus crippled, the west wind came down the canyon with an odd message to his

nose. Wahb could not clearly read the message, but it seemed to say, 'Come,' and something within him said, 'Go.' The smell of food will draw a hungry creature and disgust a gorged one. We do not know why, and all that any one can learn is that the desire springs from a need of the body. So Wahb felt drawn by what had long disgusted him, and he slouched up the mountain path, grumbling to himself and slapping savagely back at branches that chanced to switch his face.

The odd odour grew very strong; it led him where he had never been before—up a bank of whitish sand to a bench of the same colour, where there was unhealthy-looking water running down, and a kind of fog coming out of a hole. Wahb threw up his nose suspiciously—such a peculiar smell! He climbed the bench.

A snake wriggled across the sand in front. Wahb crushed it with a blow that made the near trees shiver and sent a balanced boulder toppling down, and he growled a growl that rumbled up the valley like distant thunder. Then he came to the foggy hole. It was full of water that moved gently and steamed. Wahb put in his foot, and found it was quite warm and that it felt pleasantly on his skin. He put in both feet, and little by little went in farther, causing the pool to overflow on all sides, till he was lying at full length in the warm, almost hot, sulphur-spring, and sweltering in the greenish water, while the wind drifted the steam about overhead.

There are plenty of these sulphur-springs in the Rockies, but this chanced to be the only one on Wahb's range. He lay in it for over an hour; then, feeling that he had had enough, he heaved his huge bulk up on the bank, and realized that he was feeling remarkably well and supple. The stiffness of his hind leg was gone.

He shook the water from his shaggy coat. A broad ledge in full sun-heat invited him to stretch himself out and dry. But first he reared against the nearest tree and left a mark that

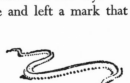

none could mistake. True, there were plenty of signs of other animals using the sulphur-bath for their ills; but what of it? Thenceforth that tree bore this inscription, in a language of mud, hair, and smell, that every mountain creature could read:

My bath. Keep away!

(signed) WAHB.

Wahb lay on his belly till his back was dry, then turned on his broad back and squirmed about in a ponderous way till the broiling sun had wholly dried him. He realized that he was really feeling very well now. He did not say to himself, 'I am troubled with that unpleasant disease called rheumatism, and sulphur-bath treatment is the thing to cure it.' But what he did know was, 'I have dreadful pains; I feel better when I am in this stinking pool.' So thenceforth he came back whenever the pains began again, and each time he was cured.

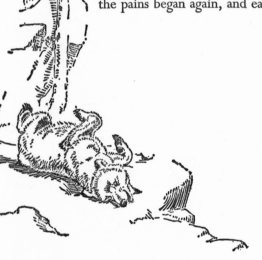

. . . he was lying . . . in the warm, almost hot, sulphur-spring . . .
(*see page 105*)

11

Y EARS went by. Wahb grew no bigger—there was no need for that—but he got whiter, crosser, and more dangerous. He really had an enormous range now. Each spring, after the winter storms had removed his notice-boards, he went around and renewed them. It was natural to do so, for, first of all, the scarcity of food compelled him to travel all over the range. There were lots of clay wallows at that season, and the itching of his skin, as the winter coat began to shed, made the dressing of cool, wet clay very pleasant, and the exquisite pain of a good scratching was one of the finest pleasures he knew. So, whatever his motive, the result was the same: the signs were renewed each spring.

At length the Palette Ranch outfit appeared on the Lower Piney, and the men got acquainted with the 'ugly old fellow.' The Cow-punchers, when they saw him, decided they 'hadn't lost any bears and they had better keep out of his way and let him mind his business.'

They did not often see him, although his tracks and

sign-boards were everywhere. But the owner of this outfit, a born hunter, took a keen interest in Wahb. He learned something of the old bear's history from Colonel Pickett, and found out for himself more than the colonel ever knew.

He learned that Wahb ranged as far south as the Upper Wiggins Fork and north to the Stinking Water, and from the Meteetsee to the Shoshones.

He found that Wahb knew more about bear-traps than most trappers do; that he either passed them by or tore open the other end of the bait-pen and dragged out the bait without going near the trap, and by accident or design Wahb sometimes sprang the trap with one of the logs that formed the pen. This ranch-owner found also that Wahb disappeared from his range each year during the heat of the summer, as completely as he did each winter during his sleep.

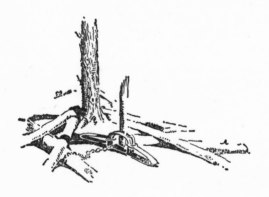

12

MANY years ago a wise government set aside the head waters of the Yellowstone to be a sanctuary of wild life forever. In the limits of this great wonderland the ideal of the royal singer was to be realized, and none were to harm or make afraid. No violence was to be offered to any bird or beast, no axe was to be carried into its primitive forests, and the streams were to flow on forever unpolluted by mill or mine. All things were to bear witness that such as this was the west before the white man came.

The wild animals quickly found out all this. They soon learned the boundaries of this unfenced park, and, as every one knows, they show a different nature within its sacred limits. They no longer shun the face of man, they neither fear nor attack him, and they are even more tolerant of one another in this land of refuge.

Peace and plenty are the sum of earthly good; so, finding them here, the wild creatures crowd into the park from the surrounding country in numbers not elsewhere to be seen.

The bears are especially numerous about the Fountain Hotel. In the woods, a quarter of a mile away, is a smooth open

place where the steward of the hotel has all the broken and waste food put out daily for the bears, and the man whose work it is has become the Steward of the Bears' Banquet. Each day it is spread, and each year there are more bears to partake of it. It is a common thing now to see a dozen bears feasting there at one time. They are of all kinds—Black, Brown, Cinnamon, Grizzly, Silvertip, Roachbacks, big and small, families and rangers, from all parts of the vast surrounding country. All seem to realize that in the park no violence is allowed, and the most ferocious of them have here put on a new behaviour. Although scores of bears roam about this choice resort, and sometimes quarrel among themselves, not one of them has ever yet harmed a man.

Year after year they have come and gone. The passing travellers see them. The men of the hotel know many of them well. They know that they show up each summer during the short season when the hotel is in use, and that they disappear again, no man knowing whence they come or whither they go.

One day the owner of the Palette Ranch came through the park. During his stay at the Fountain Hotel, he went to the Bear Banquet Hall at high meal-tide. There were several Blackbears feasting, but they made way for a huge Silvertip Grizzly that came about sundown.

'That,' said the man who was acting as guide, 'is the biggest Grizzly in the park; but he is a peaceable sort, or Lud knows what'd happen.'

'That!' said the ranchman, in astonishment, as the Grizzly came hulking nearer, and loomed up like a load of hay among the piney pillars of the Banquet Hall. 'That! If that is not Meteetsee Wahb, I never saw a bear in my life! Why, that is the worst Grizzly that ever rolled a log in the Big Horn Basin.'

'It ain't possible,' said the other, 'for he's here every summer, July and August, an' I reckon he don't live so far away.'

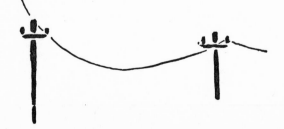

'Well, that settles it,' said the ranchman; 'July and August is just the time we miss him on the range; and you can see for yourself that he is a little lame behind and has lost a claw of his left front foot. Now I know where he puts in his summers; but I did not suppose that the old reprobate would know enough to behave himself away from home.'

The big Grizzly became very well known during the successive hotel seasons. Once only did he really behave ill, and that was the first season he appeared, before he fully knew the ways of the park.

He wandered over to the hotel, one day, and in at the front door. In the hall he reared up his eight feet of stature as the guests fled in terror; then he went into the clerk's office. The man said: 'All right; if you need this office more than I do, you can have it,' and leaping over the counter, locked himself in the telegraph-office to wire the superintendent of the park: 'Old Grizzly in the office now, seems to want to run hotel; may we shoot?'

The reply came: 'No shooting allowed in park; use the hose.' Which they did, and, wholly taken by surprise, the bear leaped over the counter too, and ambled out the back way, with a heavy *thud-thudding* of his feet, and a rattling of his claws on the floor. He passed through the kitchen as he went, and, picking up a quarter of beef, took it along.

This was the only time he was known to do ill, though on one occasion he was led into a breach of the peace by another bear. This was a large she-Blackbear and a noted mischief-maker. She had a wretched, sickly cub that she was very proud of—so proud that she went out of her way to seek trouble on his behalf. And he, like all spoiled children, was the cause of much bad feeling. She was so big and fierce that she could bully all the other Blackbears, but when she tried to drive off old Wahb she received a pat from his paw that sent her tumbling like a football. He followed her up, and would have killed

her, for she had broken the peace of the park, but she escaped by climbing a tree, from the top of which her miserable little cub was apprehensively squealing at the pitch of his voice. So the affair was ended; in future the Blackbear kept out of Wahb's way, and he won the reputation of being a peaceable, well-behaved bear. Most persons believed that he came from some remote mountains where were neither guns nor traps to make him sullen and revengeful.

13

Every one knows that a Bitter-root Grizzly is a bad bear. The Bitter-root Range is the roughest part of the mountains. The ground is everywhere cut up with deep ravines and over-grown with dense and tangled underbrush.

It is an impossible country for horses, and difficult for gunners, and there is any amount of good bear-pasture. So there are plenty of bears and plenty of trappers.

The Roachbacks, as the Bitter-root Grizzlies are called, are a cunning and desperate race. An old Roachback knows more about traps than half a dozen ordinary trappers; he knows more about plants and roots than a whole college of botanists. He can tell to a certainty just when and where to find each kind of grub and worm, and he knows by a whiff whether the hunter on his trail a mile away is working with guns, poison, dogs, traps, or all of them together. And he has one general rule, which is an endless puzzle to the hunter: 'Whatever you decide to do, do it quickly and follow it right up.' So when a trapper and a Roachback meet, the bear at once makes up his mind to run away as hard as he can, or to rush at the man and fight to a finish.

The Grizzlies of the Bad Lands did not do this: they used to stand on their dignity and growl like a thunderstorm, and so gave the hunters a chance to play their deadly lightning; and lightning is worse than thunder any day. Men can get used to growls that rumble along the ground and up one's legs to the little house where one's courage lives; but bears cannot get used to 45-90 soft-nosed bullets, and that is why the Grizzlies of the Bad Lands were all killed off.

So the hunters have learned that they never know what a Roachback will do; but they do know that he is going to be quick about it.

Altogether these Bitter-root Grizzlies have solved very well the problem of life, in spite of white men, and are therefore increasing in their own wild mountains.

Of course a range will hold only so many bears, and the increase is crowded out; so that when that slim young Bald-faced Roachback found he could not hold the range he wanted, he went out perforce to seek his fortune in the world.

He was not a big bear, or he would not have been crowded out; but he had been trained in a good school, so that he was cunning enough to get on very well elsewhere. How he wandered down to the Salmon River Mountains and did not like them; how he travelled till he got among the barb-wire fences of the Snake Plains and of course could not stay there; how a mere chance turned him from going eastward to the park, where he might have rested; how he made for the Snake River Mountains and found more hunters than berries; how he crossed into the Tetons and looked down with disgust on the teeming man colony of Jackson's Hole, does not belong to this history of Wahb. But when Baldy Roachback crossed the Gros Ventre Range and over the Wind River Divide to the head of the Greybull, he does come into the story, just as he did into the country and the life of the Meteetsee Grizzly.

The Roachback had not found a man-sign since he left

Jackson's Hole, and here he was in a land of plenty of food. He feasted on all the delicacies of the season, and enjoyed the easy, brushless country till he came on one of Wahb's sign-posts.

'Trespassers beware!' it said in the plainest manner. The Roachback reared up against it.

'Thunder! what a bear!' The nose-mark was a head and neck above Baldy's highest reach. Now, a simple bear would have gone quietly away after this discovery; but Baldy felt that the mountains owed him a living, and here was a good one if he could keep out of the way of the big fellow. He nosed about the place, kept a sharp lookout for the present owner, and went on feeding wherever he ran across a good thing.

A step or two from this ominous tree was an old pine stump. In the Bitter-roots there are often mice nests under such stumps, and Baldy jerked it over to see. There was nothing. The stump rolled over against the signpost. Baldy had not yet made up his mind about it; but a new notion came into his cunning brain. He turned his head on this side, then on that. He looked at the stump, then at the sign, with his little pig-like eyes. Then he deliberately stood up on the pine root, with his back to the tree, and put his mark away up, a head at least above that of Wahb. He rubbed his back long and hard, and he sought some mud to smear his head and shoulders, then came back and made the mark so big, so strong, and so high, and emphasized it with such claw-gashes in the bark, that it could be read only in one way—a challenge to the present claimant from some monstrous invader, who was ready, nay anxious, to fight to a finish for this desirable range.

Maybe it was accident and maybe design, but when the Roachback jumped from the root it rolled to one side. Baldy went on down the canyon, keeping the keenest lookout for his enemy.

It was not long before Wahb found the trail of the interloper, and all the ferocity of his outside-the-park nature was aroused.

He followed the trail for miles on more than one occasion. But the small bear was quick-footed as well as quick-witted and never showed himself. He made a point, however, of calling at each signpost, and if there was any means of cheating, so that his mark might be put higher, he did it with a vim, and left a big, showy record. But if there was no chance of any but a fair register, he would not go near the tree, but looked for a fresh tree near by with some log or side ledge to reach from.

Thus Wahb soon found the interloper's marks towering far above his own—a monstrous bear evidently, that even he could not be sure of mastering. But Wahb was no coward. He was ready to fight to a finish any one that might come; and he hunted the range for that invader. Day after day Wahb sought for him and held himself ready to fight. He found his trail daily, and more and more often he found that towering record far above his own. He often smelled him on the wind; but he never saw him, for the old Grizzly's eyes had grown very dim of late years; things but a little way off were mere blurs to him. The continual menace could not but fill Wahb with uneasiness, for he was not young now, and his teeth and claws were worn and blunted. He was more than ever troubled with pains in his old wounds, and though he could have risen on the spur of the moment to fight any number of Grizzlies of any size, still the continual apprehension, the knowledge that he must hold himself ready at any moment to fight this young monster, weighed on his spirits and began to tell on his general health.

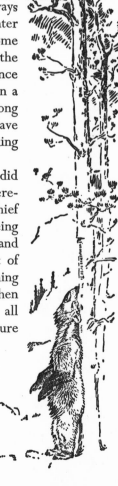

THE Roachback's life was one of continual vigilance, always ready to run, doubling and shifting to avoid the encounter that must mean instant death to him. Many a time from some hiding-place he watched the great bear, and trembled lest the wind should betray him. Several times his very impudence saved him, and more than once he was nearly cornered in a box-canyon. Once he escaped only by climbing up a long crack in a cliff, which Wahb's huge frame could not have entered. But still, in a mad persistence, he kept on marking the trees farther into the range.

At last he scented and followed up the sulphur bath. He did not understand it at all. It had no appeal to him, but hereabouts were the tracks of the owner. In a spirit of mischief the Roachback scratched dirt into the spring, and then seeing the rubbing-tree, he stood sidewise on the rocky ledge, and was thus able to put his mark fully five feet above that of Wahb. Then he nervously jumped down, and was running about, defiling the bath and keeping a sharp lookout, when he heard a noise in the woods below. Instantly he was all alert. The sound drew near, then the wind brought the sure proof, and the Roachback, in terror, turned and fled into the woods.

It was Wahb. He had been failing in health of late; his old pains were on him again, and, as well as his hind leg, had seized his right shoulder, where were still lodged two rifle-balls. He was feeling very ill, and crippled with pain. He came up the familiar bank at a jerky limp, and there caught the odour of the foe; then he saw the track in the mud—his eyes said the track of a *small* bear, but his eyes were dim now, and his nose, his unerring nose, said, 'This is the track of the huge invader.' Then he noticed the tree with his sign on it, and there beyond doubt was the stranger's mark far above his own. His eyes and nose were agreed on this; and more, they told him that the foe was close at hand, might at any moment come.

Wahb was feeling ill and weak with pain. He was in no mood for a desperate fight. A battle against such odds would be madness now. So, without taking the treatment, he turned and swung along the bench away from the direction taken by the stranger—the first time since his cubhood that he had declined to fight.

That was a turning-point in Wahb's life. If he had followed up the stranger he would have found the miserable little craven trembling, cowering, in an agony of terror, behind a log in a natural trap, a walled-in glade only fifty yards away, and would surely have crushed him. Had he even taken the bath, his strength and courage would have been renewed, and if not, then at least in time he would have met his foe, and his after life would have been different. But he had turned. This was the fork in the trail, but he had no means of knowing it.

He limped along, skirting the lower spurs of the Shoshones, and soon came on that horrid smell that he had known for years, but never followed up or understood. It was right in his road, and he traced it to a small, barren ravine that was

strewn over with skeletons and dark objects, and Wahb, as he passed, smelled a smell of many different animals, and knew by its quality that they were lying dead in this treeless, grassless hollow. For there was a cleft in the rocks at the upper end, whence poured a deadly gas; invisible but heavy, it filled the little gulch like a brimming poison bowl, and at the lower end there was a steady overflow. But Wahb knew only that the air that poured from it as he passed made him dizzy and sleepy, and repelled him, so that he got quickly away from it and was glad once more to breathe the piney wind.

Once Wahb decided to retreat, it was all too easy to do so next time; and the result worked double disaster. For, since the big stranger was allowed possession of the sulphur-spring, Wahb felt that he would rather not go there. Sometimes when he came across the traces of his foe, a spurt of his old courage would come back. He would rumble that thunder-growl as of old, and go painfully lumbering along the trail to settle the thing right then and there. But he never overtook the mysterious giant, and his rheumatism, growing worse now that he was barred from the cure, soon made him daily less capable of either running or fighting.

Sometimes Wahb would sense his foe's approach when he was in a bad place for fighting, and, without really running, he would yield to a wish to be on a better footing, where he would have a fair chance. This better footing never led him nearer the enemy, for it is well known that the one awaiting has the advantage.

Some days Wahb felt so ill that it would have been madness to have staked everything on a fight, and when he felt well or a little better, the stranger seemed to keep away.

Wahb soon found that the stranger's track was most often on the Warhouse and the west slope of the Piney, the very best feeding-grounds. To avoid these when he did not feel equal to fighting was only natural, and as he was always in more or less pain now, it amounted to abandoning to the stranger the best part of the range.

Weeks went by. Wahb had meant to go back to his bath, but he never did. His pains grew worse; he was now crippled in his right shoulder as well as in his hind leg.

The long strain of waiting for the fight begot anxiety, that grew to be apprehension, which, with the sapping of his strength, was breaking down his courage, as it always must when courage is founded on muscular force. His daily care now was not to meet and fight the invader, but to avoid him till he felt better.

Thus that first little retreat grew into one long retreat. Whab had to go farther and farther down the Piney to avoid an encounter. He was daily worse fed, and as the weeks went by was daily less able to crush a foe.

He was living and hiding at last on the Lower Piney—the very place where once his mother had brought him with his little brothers. The life he led now was much like the one he had led after that dark day. Perhaps for the same reason. If he had had a family of his own all might have been different. As he limped along one morning, seeking among the barren aspen groves for a few roots, or the wormy partridge-berries that were too poor to interest the squirrel and the grouse, he heard a stone rattle down the western slope into the woods, and, a little later, on the wind was borne the dreaded taint. He waded through the ice-cold Piney—once he would have leaped it—and the chill water sent through and up each great hairy limb keen pains that seemed to reach his very life. He was retreating again—which way? There seemed but one way now—towards the new ranch-house.

But there were signs of stir about it long before he was near enough to be seen. His nose, his trustiest friend, said, 'Turn, turn and seek the hills,' and turn he did even at the risk of meeting there the dreadful foe. He limped painfully along the north bank of the Piney, keeping in the hollows and among the trees. He tried to climb a cliff that of old he had often bounded up at full speed. When half-way up his footing gave way, and down he rolled to the bottom. A long way round was now the only road, for onward he must go—on—on. But where? There seemed no choice now but to abandon the whole range to the terrible stranger.

And feeling, as far as a bear can feel, that he is fallen, defeated, dethroned at last, that he is driven from his ancient range by a bear too strong for him to face, he turned up the west fork, and the lot was drawn. The strength and speed were gone from his once mighty limbs; he took three times as long as he once would to mount each well-known ridge, and as he went he glanced backwards from time to time to know if he were pursued. Away up the head of the little branch were the Shoshones, bleak, forbidding; no enemies were there, and the park was beyond it all—on, on he must go. But as he climbed with shaky limbs, and short uncertain steps, the west wind brought the odour of Death Gulch, that fearful little valley where everything was dead, where the very air was deadly. It used to disgust him and drive him away, but now Wahb felt that it had a message for him; he was drawn by it. It was in his line of flight, and he hobbled slowly towards the place. He went nearer, nearer, until he stood upon the entering ledge. A vulture that had descended to feed on one of the victims was slowly going to sleep on the untouched carcass. Wahb swung his great grizzled muzzle and his long white beard in the wind. The odour that he once had hated was attractive now. There was a strange biting quality in the air. His body craved it. For it seemed to numb his pain and it promised sleep, as it did that day when first he saw the place.

Far below him, to the right and to the left and on and on as far as the eye could reach, was the great kingdom that once had been his; where he had lived for years in the glory of his strength; where none had dared to meet him face to face. The whole earth could show no view more beautiful. But Wahb had no thought of its beauty; he only knew that it was a good land to live in; that it had been his, but that now it was gone, for his strength was gone, and he was flying to seek a place where he could rest and be at peace.

Away over the Shoshones, indeed, was the road to the park, but it was far, far away, with a doubtful end to the long, doubtful journey. But why so far? Here in this little gulch was all he sought; here were peace and painless sleep. He knew it; for his nose, his never-erring nose, said, '*Here! here now!*'

He paused a moment at the gate, and as he stood the wind-borne fumes began their subtle work. Five were the faithful wardens of his life, and the best and trustiest of them all flung open wide the door he long had kept. A moment still Wahb stood in doubt. His lifelong guide was silent now, had given up his post. But another sense he felt within. The Angel of the Wild Things was standing there, beckoning, in the little vale. Wahb did not understand. He had no eyes to see the tear in the angel's eyes, nor the pitying smile that was surely on his lips. He could not even see the angel. But he *felt* him beckoning, beckoning.

A rush of his ancient courage surged in the Grizzly's rugged breast. He turned aside into the little gulch. The deadly vapours entered in, filled his huge chest and tingled in his vast, heroic limbs as he calmly lay down on the rocky, herbless floor and as gently went to sleep, as he did that day in his mother's arms by the Greybull, long ago.

Titles in this Series of Illustrated Classics

CHILDREN'S ILLUSTRATED CLASSICS

(Illustrated Classics for Older Readers are listed on fourth page)

Andrew Lang's ADVENTURES OF ODYSSEUS. Illustrated by KIDDELL-MONROE.

AESOP'S FABLES. Illustrated by KIDDELL-MONROE.

Lewis Carroll's ALICE'S ADVENTURES IN WONDERLAND and THROUGH THE LOOKING-GLASS. Illustrated by JOHN TENNIEL.

George MacDonald's AT THE BACK OF THE NORTH WIND. Illustrated by E. H. SHEPARD.

Robert Louis Stevenson's THE BLACK ARROW. Illustrated by LIONEL EDWARDS.

Anna Sewell's BLACK BEAUTY. Illustrated by LUCY KEMP-WELCH.

Roger Lancelyn Green's A BOOK OF MYTHS. Illustrated by KIDDELL-MONROE.

THE BOOK OF NONSENSE. Edited by ROGER LANCELYN GREEN. Illustrated by CHARLES FOLKARD in colour, and with original drawings by TENNIEL, LEAR, FURNISS, HOLIDAY, HUGHES, SHEPARD and others.

THE BOOK OF VERSE FOR CHILDREN. Collected by ROGER LANCELYN GREEN. Illustrated with two-colour drawings in the text by MARY SHILLABEER. (Not available in the U.S.A. in this edition.)

Mrs Ewing's THE BROWNIES AND OTHER STORIES. Illustrated by E. H. SHEPARD.

Mrs Molesworth's THE CARVED LIONS. Illustrated by LEWIS HART.

Captain Marryat's THE CHILDREN OF THE NEW FOREST. Illustrated by LIONEL EDWARDS.

Robert Louis Stevenson's A CHILD'S GARDEN OF VERSES. Illustrated by MARY SHILLABEER.

Charles Dickens's A CHRISTMAS CAROL and THE CRICKET ON THE HEARTH. Illustrated by C. E. BROCK.

R. M. Ballantyne's THE CORAL ISLAND. Illustrated by LEO BATES.

Mrs Molesworth's THE CUCKOO CLOCK. Illustrated by E. H. SHEPARD.

Jean Webster's DADDY-LONG-LEGS. Illustrated by HENRY FAIRBAIRN.

R. M. Ballantyne's **THE DOG CRUSOE.** Illustrated by VICTOR AMBRUS.

E. Nesbit's **THE ENCHANTED CASTLE.** Illustrated by CECIL LESLIE.

FAIRY TALES FROM THE ARABIAN NIGHTS. Illustrated by KIDDELL-MONROE.

FAIRY TALES OF LONG AGO. Edited by M. C. CAREY. Illustrated by D. J. WATKINS-PITCHFORD.

Louisa M. Alcott's **GOOD WIVES.** Illustrated by S. VAN ABBÉ.

Frances Browne's **GRANNY'S WONDERFUL CHAIR.** Illustrated by D. J. WATKINS-PITCHFORD.

GRIMMS' FAIRY TALES. Illustrated by CHARLES FOLKARD.

HANS ANDERSEN'S FAIRY TALES. Illustrated by HANS BAUMHAUER.

Mary Mapes Dodge's **HANS BRINKER.** Illustrated by HANS BAUMHAUER.

Oscar Wilde's **THE HAPPY PRINCE AND OTHER STORIES.** Illustrated by PEGGY FORTNUM.

Johanna Spyri's **HEIDI.** Illustrated by VINCENT O. COHEN.

Charles Kingsley's **THE HEROES.** Illustrated by KIDDELL-MONROE.

Edith Nesbit's **THE HOUSE OF ARDEN.** Illustrated by CLARKE HUTTON.

Mark Twain's **HUCKLEBERRY FINN**

TOM SAWYER
Both illustrated by C. WALTER HODGES.

Louisa M. Alcott's **JO'S BOYS.** Illustrated by HARRY TOOTHILL.

A. M. Hadfield's **KING ARTHUR AND THE ROUND TABLE.** Illustrated by DONALD SETON CAMMELL.

Charlotte M. Yonge's **THE LITTLE DUKE.** Illustrated by MICHAEL GODFREY.

Frances Hodgson Burnett's **LITTLE LORD FAUNTLEROY.**

Louisa M. Alcott's **LITTLE MEN.** Illustrated by HARRY TOOTHILL.

LITTLE WOMEN. Illustrated by S. VAN ABBÉ.

Mrs Ewing's **LOB LIE-BY-THE-FIRE** and **THE STORY OF A SHORT LIFE.** Illustrated by RANDOLPH CALDECOTT ('Lob') and H. M. BROCK ('Short Life').

MODERN FAIRY STORIES. Edited by ROGER LANCELYN GREEN. Illustrated by E. H. SHEPARD.

Jean Ingelow's **MOPSA THE FAIRY.** Illustrated by DORA CURTIS.

NURSERY RHYMES. Collected and illustrated in two-colour line by A. H. WATSON.

Carlo Collodi's **PINOCCHIO.** The Story of a Puppet. Illustrated by CHARLES FOLKARD.

Mark Twain's **THE PRINCE AND THE PAUPER.** Illustrated by ROBERT HODGSON.

Andrew Lang's **PRINCE PRIGIO** and **PRINCE RICARDO.** Illustrated by D. J. WATKINS-PITCHFORD.

George MacDonald's **THE LOST PRINCESS**

THE PRINCESS AND CURDIE

THE PRINCESS AND THE GOBLIN
The first two volumes illustrated by CHARLES FOLKARD, the third by D. J. WATKINS-PITCHFORD.

Carola Oman's **ROBIN HOOD.** Illustrated by S. VAN ABBÉ.

W. M. Thackeray's **THE ROSE AND THE RING** and Charles Dickens's **THE MAGIC FISH-BONE.**
Two children's stories, the first containing the author's illustrations, the latter containing PAUL HOGARTH'S work.

H. W. Longfellow's **THE SONG OF HIAWATHA** Illustrated by KIDDELL-MONROE.

J. R. Wyss's **THE SWISS FAMILY ROBINSON.** Illustrated by CHARLES FOLKARD.

Charles and Mary Lamb's **TALES FROM SHAKESPEARE.** Illustrated by ARTHUR RACKHAM.

TALES OF MAKE-BELIEVE. Edited by ROGER LANCELYN GREEN. Illustrated by HARRY TOOTHILL.
Charles Dickens, Rudyard Kipling, E. Nesbit, Thomas Hardy, E. V. Lucas, etc.

Nathaniel Hawthorne's **TANGLEWOOD TALES.** Illustrated by S. VAN ABBÉ.

Thomas Hughes's **TOM BROWN'S SCHOOLDAYS.** Illustrated by S. VAN ABBÉ.

Charles Kingsley's **THE WATER-BABIES.** Illustrated by ROSALIE K. FRY.

Susan Coolidge's **WHAT KATY DID.** Illustrated by MARGERY GILL.

Nathaniel Hawthorne's **A WONDER BOOK.** Illustrated by S. VAN ABBÉ.

Selma Lagerlöf's **THE WONDERFUL ADVENTURES OF NILS.**

THE FURTHER ADVENTURES OF NILS.
Both illustrated by HANS BAUMHAUER

Illustrated Classics for Older Readers

Jack London's **THE CALL OF THE WILD.** Illustrated by CHARLES PICKARD.

Cervantes's **DON QUIXOTE.** (Edited) Illustrated by W. HEATH ROBINSON.

Jonathan Swift's **GULLIVER'S TRAVELS.** (Edited) Illustrated by ARTHUR RACKHAM.

R. L. Stevenson's **KIDNAPPED.** Illustrated by G. OAKLEY.

H. Rider Haggard **KING SOLOMON'S MINES.** Illustrated by A. R. WHITEAR.

Frank L. Baum's **THE MARVELLOUS LAND OF OZ**

        THE WONDERFUL WIZARD OF OZ
Both illustrated by B. S. BIRO.

John Bunyan's **THE PILGRIM'S PROGRESS.** Illustrated by FRANK C. PAPÉ.

Anthony Hope's **THE PRISONER OF ZENDA.** Illustrated by MICHAEL GODFREY.

Erskine Childers's **THE RIDDLE OF THE SANDS.** Illustrated by CHARLES MOZLEY.

Daniel Defoe's **ROBINSON CRUSOE.** Illustrated by J. AYTON SYMINGTON.

Anthony Hope's **RUPERT OF HENTZAU.** Illustrated by MICHAEL GODFREY.

TEN TALES OF DETECTION. Edited by ROGER LANCELYN GREEN. Illustrated by IAN RIBBONS.

Roger Lancelyn Green's **THE TALE OF ANCIENT ISRAEL.** Illustrated by CHARLES KEEPING.

THIRTEEN UNCANNY TALES. Illustrated by RAY OGDEN.
    F. Anstey, M. R. James, Sir Arthur Conan Doyle, H. G. Wells and others.

John Buchan **THE THIRTY-NINE STEPS.** Illustrated by EDWARD ARDIZZONE.

Ernest Thompson Seton's **THE TRAIL OF THE SANDHILL STAG and Other** Lives of the Hunted. Illustrated with drawings by the author and coloured frontispiece by RITA PARSONS.

Robert Louis Stevenson's **TREASURE ISLAND.** Illustrated by S. VAN ABBÉ.

Jules Verne's **AROUND THE MOON**

        AROUND THE WORLD IN EIGHTY DAYS

        FROM THE EARTH TO THE MOON

        JOURNEY TO THE CENTRE OF THE EARTH
All illustrated by W. F. PHILLIPPS.

        TWENTY THOUSAND LEAGUES UNDER THE SEA
Illustrated by WILLIAM MCLAREN.

Jack London's **WHITE FANG.** Illustrated by CHARLES PICKARD.

Further volumes in preparation